FARAH'S PILOT

A NOVEL

CHARLES THOMAS

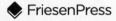 FriesenPress

One Printers Way
Altona, MB R0G 0B0
Canada

www.friesenpress.com

ISBN
978-1-03-913959-6 (Hardcover)
978-1-03-913958-9 (Paperback)
978-1-03-913960-2 (eBook)

1. *FICTION, ROMANCE, MULTICULTURAL & INTERRACIAL*

Distributed to the trade by The Ingram Book Company

FARAH'S PILOT

CHAPTER 1

aptain Xavier Sutton and his wife Farah were staring up at the large information screen that listed the flight departure times for June 30, 2020. Xavier tapped Farah lightly on the arm and informed her that his Marseilles flight was on schedule. Since the Kuala Lumpur traffic had been much lighter than normal, they had arrived at the airport with plenty of time to spare before Xavier needed to head to his departure gate.

Xavier went to the Air France counter to check in his bag and to collect his boarding pass while Farah went to find an open table at one of the many coffee shops on the departure level, where they could sit down and enjoy each other's company before Xavier had to depart.

As they sat and enjoyed their coffee and fresh-baked pastries, Farah asked Xavier if he had remembered to pack his essentials and reminded him about the envelope of Euros and the two packs of Vitamin C tablets that she had put in his carry-on bag. Farah could tell from the way that Xavier nodded his head to acknowledge her comments that he was preoccupied with other thoughts, and she assumed that they were the same negative thoughts that he had previously expressed to her regarding his air force work. His job, currently, was to assess and recommend a vendor for their new fighter jet aircraft. Xavier's trip to Marseille was for a second technical review of the Delorme Aviation Vitesse jet, which was one of two fighter jet options being considered by the Royal Malaysian Air Force. Over the past six months he had expressed his concerns to Farah, that certain unknown parties within the Malaysian government, and perhaps even within the military, were trying to unfairly influence the air force's decision on purchasing new fighter jets in favour of the French vendor. Xavier and Farah both despised the endemic corruption that existed within the government and its ministries, and that was why Xavier had formally rejected the offer that he had received a few months earlier, from the Ministry of Defence. The offer that Xavier had received was to train for two years with an elite jet fighter squadron within the French Air Force, while Farah worked on a two-year assignment with the Paris based IMF organization. They had both concluded that the offer was linked to the efforts being made by certain parties on behalf of the French, to secure Xavier's positive technical assessment for their jets.

Farah gently grabbed a hold of Xavier's arm, made sure that he was looking at her, and reminded him that the reason he had joined the air force was his passion for flying. Then she told him that he should go to Marseilles and focus on the enjoyment of flying the French jets, and to forget about all the things that he couldn't control.

Xavier thanked Farah for bringing him back to reality, and he assured her that he would enjoy his trip, and that he would undertake his air force assignment with a clear mind and with a clean conscience.

Sensing that Xavier was in a better frame of mind, Farah asked him if he had the piece of paper that she had given him, which had the model number and the colour of the French-made handbag that she wanted him to buy for her at the Marseilles Duty Free. As he went into the side pocket of his carry-on, presumably to retrieve the paper, she emphasized to him that he should not buy any other model if her choice wasn't available.

Xavier leaned closer to Farah as he showed her the paper that she had been referring to, and then he softly told her that if they didn't have the bag that she wanted in Marseilles, then he would fly to Paris, or even London to find it. Upon hearing this, Farah reached over and softly put her hand on top of his, and then she gave him one of her wonderful smiles. Xavier was now looking directly into Farah's eyes when he told her that she looked as amazing as she always did, and that he loved how she looked with her hair pulled back. Farah had an appreciative smile on her face when she told him to stop being stupid; she then reminded him that she had only put her hair back because she was too rushed to do anything else. Farah took a quick glance at the large clock on the wall, before suggesting to Xavier that he should go, and then they proceeded to the security checkpoint in front of the escalator that would take Xavier down to the customs and immigration level. Xavier kissed Farah, told her that he loved her very much, then turned to present his passport to the immigration officer before stepping onto the downward-moving escalator. Once his passport had been checked and stamped at the immigration counter, Xavier took one final look up at the departure level, and he was relieved to see that Farah was looking down at him with her wonderful smile. They waved a final goodbye.

XAVIER ADMIRED THE overall beauty of the city of Marseilles as he looked out the coach bus window on the ride from the airport to the InterContinental Hotel in the city centre. He recalled his previous trip to Marseilles, how he had been so impressed with the layout of the city, with its many ports and harbours facing the majestic Mediterranean, and with the many cliffs and hillsides acting as a protective backdrop.

As the bus got closer to the city centre, Xavier could see the impressive white roof structure of the Olympique de Marseilles soccer stadium, which was widely recognized by soccer fans throughout Europe, and which was frequented and adored by the soccer-crazed citizens of Marseilles. The city competed with Paris on the soccer pitch, and for the bragging rights of which city was more important to France, both in the past and in the present. Marseilles, in addition to being the second-largest city in France, also was the country's largest commercial port, and it had a very rich and proud history. The city had played a leading role in the creation of the French Republic and was also the birthplace of the French national anthem, "La Marseillaise." Xavier had told Farah that he would like to bring her to Marseilles one day, so that they could explore the city and its unknown mysteries. The combination of the traditional French influences and those of the North African countries and bordering Europeon countries created a unique potpourri of both peoples and cultures.

As Xavier waited his turn to get off the bus, he remembered the observations he had made at the boarding gate in Kuala Lumpur, where it had seemed to him that there were more government ministry personnel than usual on this official visit to Delorme Aviation. This heightened his suspicions that vested interests might be involved, as he was under the impression that the trip was for technical evaluation reasons. Before he got too carried away with his thoughts, he remembered what Farah had told him at the airport, and with her comments in mind, he turned his focus to the enjoyment he would get when he got to fly the French Vitesse jet.

Xavier and others from the Malaysian delegation were met by the hotel's front desk personnel, who handed them their pre-arranged room cards. Upon receiving them, most of them, including Xavier, went directly to their rooms, likely wanting to relax and refresh before the evening dinner that was being hosted by the owner of Delorme Aviation.

LATER THAT DAY, Xavier stepped off the elevator on the concourse level of the hotel, immediately spotting the sign indicating the location of the Delorme Aviation dinner. He was in his full military dress, which included the impressive white dress jacket displaying his military insignia and rank designation, and as he stood there looking into the function room, he could have easily been mistaken for the leading actor in some Hollywood production. Xavier had been blessed with a beautiful olive complexion, a distinctive feature from his mother's Eurasian heritage, and that attractive skin tone was complimented by the traditionally handsome features he had inherited from his Canadian father.

It was easy for Xavier to distinguish how many civilians were in attendance when he looked at the crowd assembled outside the function room, as their dark, western-style suits provided a stark contrast to the white uniforms of the air force members. Xavier easily located his fellow pilot, Lt. Colonel Lim, and he made his away across the room to say hello, and to reminisce about their previous trip to Marseilles, and about some of their weekends on the beach with Lim's wife and Xavier's architect friend.

Lim asked Xavier what he thought of the lovely young ladies that were mingling amongst the crowd, and surprisingly, Xavier had to acknowledge to him that he had not really taken much notice of them. But then he started to take a closer look. They both agreed that these women looked stunning in their matching, form-fitting blue dresses, and that they were a welcome addition to the boring Malaysian ministry officials, and the various Delorme Aviation personnel.

Xavier estimated the age of the ladies as somewhere in their mid-twenties, and he suggested to Lim that they looked like they were of either Moroccan or Algerian descent. The fact that these young ladies would be from one of those countries would not be rare, since France had a large and growing population of immigrants from the North African countries, and they were becoming more prevalent in French society. Unfortunately, as would have been evident to the Malaysians, almost every person providing the low-paying services along their travels, either when they got on their bus from the airport, or when they arrived at their hotel, was an immigrant. The traditional French citizens seemed quite content to have their under-appreciated immigrants handling the menial jobs in their towns and cities, while they maintained their firm grip on the easier, more lucrative jobs.

Lim advised Xavier that he had better watch himself around all these beautiful women, since he was a recently married man, and his wife, Farah, would expect nothing less of her distinguished captain from the Royal Malaysian Air Force. Xavier thanked Lim for his thoughtful reminders, and then he assured him that Farah was uppermost in his mind, including this evening.

One of the Delorme Aviation staff announced to the crowd that everyone should take their seats at their designated tables, as the dinner was about to commence. Xavier had noticed some extra activity taking place outside the function room, and when he took a closer, he saw that an elderly man with silver hair was surrounded by people. As it turned out, the silver-haired man was indeed Mr. Jacques Delorme, the president and majority shareholder of Delorme Aviation.

While he was waiting for the first course to arrive, Xavier took a closer look at the printed menu card in front of him, and he was impressed to see the small Halal designation at the bottom of the card, indicating that the dinner menu had been prepared in compliance with Muslim dietary guidelines. Xavier thought, as he looked at the card, that Delorme Aviation was being very respectful of the fact that most of the members in the Malaysian delegation were Muslim, including himself.

Everyone at Xavier's table was discussing how wonderful the multi-course meal had been, when the host, Mr. Delorme, made his way to the lectern to deliver his dinner speech. The guests, Xavier included, tried to stifle their laughter as they listened to the Frenchman stumble through the welcoming portion of his speech in the Malay language. But as Xavier and the others at his table agreed, aside from the friendly humour that he provided, Mr. Delorme had displayed a genuine effort to show respect to them. His speech then transitioned to the more comfortable English, and as he spoke in a very clear and understandable fashion, Mr. Delorme informed his Malaysian guests of his company's recent success in delivering, ahead of schedule, the first portion of their large fighter jet order to the Egyptian government. His reference to another Muslim country being a customer of Delorme Aviation was not lost on anyone in the room that evening. In fact, it should have been evident to anyone who was attending the dinner that Delorme Aviation was sparing no effort to impress their Malaysian guests, whether it was with the excellent food, the impressive hostesses, or even with the speech—including the broken Malay portion—by their company owner.

Lim had enjoyed the meal as much as anyone at the table, but he complained to Xavier about the fact that their table did not get to enjoy the pleasure of having one of the lovely hostesses sitting with them. Xavier laughed and reminded Lim that he also was married to a very lovely lady, and that she would also expect him to uphold the high standards of an officer in the Royal Malaysian Air Force.

As they were both enjoying a good laugh, the Malaysian delegation's leader rose from his chair, and prepared to make a short speech of his own. Before he could start speaking, some of the air force men yelled out, *"En français, en français"*—but the leader showed no indication that he was going to attempt what the Delorme leader had done, as he proceeded with his comments in English. After he thanked the Delorme Aviation company for the wonderful dinner and for their genuine hospitality, he reminded his Malaysian contingent that the time was approaching ten o'clock, and that they had an early start to the day tomorrow. As military men, the attendees were very familiar with orders from their superior officers, so it was no surprise to see the multitude of white-jacketed men making their way to the elevators that would take them to their rooms.

Xavier told Lim that he was exhausted from the long day, which he reminded him had started at 5:30 a.m. in Kuala Lumpur, and that he would look forward to seeing him in the lobby restaurant for breakfast.

THE HOTEL SECURITY officer looked at his watch and saw that it was 3:00 a.m. as he slid his master key card into the guest suite door to allow the two Marseilles Police gendarmes to enter the suite.

The lights, both in the living area and in the bedroom, were on and everything looked quite normal to the gendarmes, based on their first observations. They saw a lady's dress draped over the back of one of the chairs in the living area, a pair of lady's briefs and a bra beside the chair, and a pair of high-heeled shoes on the other side of the chair. The one gendarme suggested to his partner that it looked as if the lady had been in a hurry to get somewhere.

When they entered the suite's bedroom, they found a young lady and the registered room guest, Captain Sutton, lying naked on the bed—neither of them responding to any of the noises in the room. The gendarmes quickly moved to the bodies to determine if there were signs of life, and they were relieved to see, from the slow movements of the subjects' chests, that they were alive and breathing. They proceeded to yell, and when that did not produce any response, they proceeded to clap their hands, but still there was no reaction. The gendarmes concluded that they were likely under the influence of some type of heavy sedative drug. They decided to contact their police headquarters to request a detective squad, then remained at the scene until the detectives arrived to take over. The detectives were the most qualified to investigate this type of crime scene, according to the established police procedures and guidelines.

Senior Detective Dube was joined by one of the department's junior detectives, and his first order of business was to request a briefing from the gendarmes on scene. After they had brought him up to speed, he advised them to secure the entire floor, and then to wait at the lobby level for the arrival of the forensic and medical teams. Both detectives then put on their rubber gloves and started their investigation in the living area, where they found the underwear and the dress. Detective Dube noticed that there were abandoned hairs in the briefs, which he retrieved with his plastic tweezers, before placing them into an evidence envelope. When he turned the briefs over, he found a room key card, which he also put in an envelope, and then after seeing that there was no other evidence in the living room area, he proceeded to the bedroom.

He first went to the young lady's side of the bed, where he did a visual review of her body, and he noted to his junior that the only signs of trauma that he could see were some minor red marks on the inner parts of her thighs. He crouched over to determine if there was any trauma evident in the vaginal region, but he found that the young lady's private area was hidden by her full, natural growth. What detective Dube then noted to the junior detective was that both the young lady's face and her hair looked untouched, and he advised his junior that they were not consistent with how a young lady would look if she had just gone through a sexual assault.

Before moving over to look at the male body, the detective noticed something in the centre of the young lady's chest, just below her breasts, and after moving closer he could see that it was a small, full-colour tattoo of a tree. He was almost certain that he had seen that specific tree design before, but he couldn't remember where, so he asked his junior to take a closer look. It did not take the junior detective long to confirm that the tree was very similar to the green cedar tree found on the Lebanese flag. Detective Dube made a note of that in his note pad before moving over to examine the male body. He noted to the junior detective that there were no signs of any trauma on his body. Captain Sutton's left arm hung over the side of the bed. When the detective kneeled to look at his hand, he found a cellphone on the carpet, which he promptly bagged into evidence, and then put in his pocket.

While the detectives waited for the arrival of the forensic team, they reviewed what they had found in the suite. Detective Dube's perspective, which came with over thirty years of experience, was that it was a staged scene. As he explained to his junior, there were no drugs or alcohol or any other substances present, and there was no evidence of any fluid or discharge on either the sheets or on the young lady. The most significant factor for Detective Dube, as he explained to his junior, was that the young lady appeared as though she had been placed in the position that they had found her in, and this led him to believe that there was a third party involved.

Detective Dube walked around, looking very impatient, while they awaited the arrival of the forensic team. He told the other detective that he wanted to cover the young lady's body, but he couldn't until the forensic team had completed their work.

When the forensic team arrived, they apologized to the detectives for the delay, explaining to them that they had been finishing another crime scene when the call came in. They asked if there were any special circumstances they should know about. Detective Dube asked them to get a good picture of the tattoo in the centre of the young lady's chest, and he also requested for them to cover the bodies as soon as they were finished. The team did not waste any time in their processing of the scene, or in taking the required pictures, before allowing the medical team to take over. After ensuring that the young lady's and Captain

Sutton's vital signs were stable, the medical team put them on the ambulance gurneys and wheeled them out of the room for immediate transport to the local hospital.

CHAPTER 2

ajor Rashid knew that he had set his alarm for 6:30 a.m., but he could see from the desk clock beside his bed that the time was 6:00 a.m., and he wondered who could be calling him at this early hour. When the head of Delorme Aviation's security department asked him if they could meet in the lobby coffee shop in thirty minutes, the major had a strong sense that something significant had taken place.

Mr. Beliveau introduced himself to the major, as he had never met the Malaysian delegation head, but he acknowledged to the major that he recognized him from the dinner. The waiter poured fresh-brewed coffee into their cups, while Mr. Beliveau tried to break the news about Captain Sutton to the major in as gentle a manner as he could. Unfortunately for Mr. Beliveau, the facts in the case involving Captain Sutton were difficult to downplay, and as such, he was unable to prevent the major from reacting with the combination of both anger and disbelief that he displayed.

After picking up his coffee spoon, which had fallen when he slammed the table, the major stated, very emphatically, to Mr.

13

Beliveau that he wanted to see Captain Sutton. Mr. Beliveau politely informed him that Captain Sutton was in the hospital undergoing tests and receiving treatments, and that it would only be later in the day that a visit would be possible.

The major was somewhat relieved, however, when he was informed that Captain Sutton was in good health, aside from the after-effects of the sedatives that were found in his system. The major was anxious to learn more about what had transpired in Captain Sutton's hotel room and frustrated to learn from Mr. Beliveau that he could not provide him with any additional information. Mr. Beliveau did, however, advise him that his department had confirmed with the Marseilles police that they would attend at the hotel to provide a full briefing, sometime later in the day.

Major Rashid thanked him for the update and left the coffee shop. As he was making his way to the lobby, Mr. Beliveau caught up to him and suggested that he delegate one of his other officers to accompany the team going to the company's facilities, so that he would be available for any meetings or updates. The major nodded his approval to his suggestion and then proceeded to his room, where he intended to contact his superior officers in Kuala Lumpur. The telephone call to his commanding officer was not a call that Major Rashid was looking forward to making, but he needed to know when he could contact Captain Sutton's wife to advise her of her husband's situation.

Over the phone, the commanding officer advised the major that he should wait until he had received the briefing from the Marseilles police before phoning Captain Sutton's wife.

Major Rashid could see that the hotel business centre was very quiet as he walked to the room that Delorme Aviation had booked for his meeting with the Marseilles police. Inside the room, he found a side table with carafes of coffee and a tray of pastries, and since there were still ten minutes before the meeting was to begin, he decided to pour himself a cup while he waited.

Shortly after sitting down with his coffee and his croissant, Mr. Beliveau and the two detectives from the Marseilles police arrived, and after they had poured themselves some coffee, the lead detective, Detective Dube, commenced the briefing. Detective Dube advised Major Rashid that Captain Sutton was in the hospital, where he was still being monitored for the effects of the heavy concentrations of the powerful sedative Rohypnol found in his body, but that he was generally in good health.

The major was noticeably relieved when the detective informed him that he was now free to visit Captain Sutton in the hospital, whenever he chose to do so. With respect to the young lady, the detective confirmed that her name was Amina Chafak, and that she also had heavy concentrations of the same sedative in her body. He informed the major that she was also in good health, but that she had sustained some minor injuries from what the medical examiner had classified as a sexual assault. The positive news: Miss Chafak was well enough to be discharged, and she was being taken to a private facility by her employer.

Major Rashid looked over at Mr. Beliveau and told him he was pleased to hear that Delorme took such good care of its employees.

Mr. Beliveau shook his head and clarified to the major that the young lady was employed by a PR agency in Paris, and that she had been at the Delorme dinner as a member of a group that had been contracted by one of Delorme's sales agents.

When the major pressed for more clarity on the sexual assault classification, Detective Dube explained that the medical team had concluded that the young lady had been penetrated, and that she had sustained sufficient internal trauma to support their finding.

Major Rashid, upset, told the detective very firmly that he didn't see how it was possible for Captain Sutton to have sexually assaulted the young lady, when he had been incapacitated by the same sedative drugs. The detective told him they had retrieved photos from Captain Sutton's cellphone, which showed Miss Chafak in some very intimate poses, including one photo that included Captain Sutton. At this, Major Rashid was silenced. His disappointment was evident to the others in the room, as he slumped back in his chair. The detective went on to say that it was in the hands of the prosecutor's office to determine if any charges would be laid against Captain Sutton, but he suggested to the major that he should be prepared for either sexual assault or rape charges, in view of the photos found on the captain's cellphone.

The major was clearly devastated at this point. He asked the detective why the police had entered Captain Sutton's room in the first place. It seemed to him that the whole situation was an obvious set up job. The detective told him that a call had been made to the hotel front desk, stating that one of the young ladies from the dinner had gone missing, and that this had led the hotel security to check their CCTV footage, where they discovered that both Captain Sutton and Miss Chafak had exited the elevator on the eighteenth floor at the same time. They had each gone their own way to their separate rooms, but since they had no other leads the hotel security officer had decided to phone Captain Sutton's room, to see if he could provide them with any information that might help them locate the missing Miss Chafak. After multiple calls to the room and repeated knocking at the door, without any response, hotel security made the decision to call the police, and when they arrived, they entered the room.

After the detective confirmed that he was not able to share any additional information at this time, Major Rashid thanked him for his briefing, and then he excused himself from the room. Before the major left the business centre, Mr. Beliveau advised him that he had arranged for a company car and driver to be placed on standby at the hotel, and that they were for his use as and when he needed them. The major thanked him as he hurried to his hotel room, so that he could phone and update his commanding officer in Kuala Lumpur, and to receive his further instructions.

After listening to the briefing from Major Rashid, the commanding officer advised the major to allow Captain Sutton to phone his wife from his hospital room, while he remained present, and then to speak to her, once their conversation finished, and to answer any questions she may have. The major was also advised to phone Captain Sutton's parents to provide them with a full briefing on everything.

THE GENDARME SITTING outside Xavier's hospital room was a stark reminder to Major Rashid of the seriousness of the situation his young captain was in. Before entering the room, the major was advised by the head nurse on the floor that Captain Sutton had had some wrist restraints put on him, as he had been very agitated, and he had attempted to leave the room more than once.

Xavier looked relieved when he saw the major enter his room, but he did not extend a proper form of greeting to him. Instead, he immediately asked him what had happened, and why he was being held in the hospital room. He said that nobody would tell him anything, and that he wanted to phone his wife to tell her that he was okay. Xavier listened while the major provided a summary of what had happened, including his opinion of how serious the situation was. Afterwards, Xavier looked absolutely dumbfounded. When he had gathered himself, he started shouting that he was being set up by people who were supporting the French jet supplier.

The major was very aware of Xavier's specific concerns regarding the fighter jet contract, and he was also aware that he had previously expressed those concerns to his commanding officer in Malaysia. After Xavier had calmed down, the major handed him his cellphone, and asked him to phone his wife, to update her on what was taking place. He suggested to Xavier that he assure her that he was healthy, and that he was being well looked after.

Farah's happiness when she received the call from her dear Xavier quickly turned to concern when he explained to her where he was and what he had been suspected of doing. Farah was horrified to learn what he had been accused of. She knew her husband and trusted him completely; she knew immediately he was innocent, that this was a set-up.

After some minutes had transpired, the major asked Xavier to close out the call so that he could speak to Farah and provide her with a better understanding of what to expect moving forward.

Farah was mid-sentence, telling Xavier that she would be travelling to Marseilles at the absolute earliest time that she could get a flight, when Major Rashid, who had retrieved his phone from Xavier, started speaking. He strongly suggested to Farah that she start looking for a good lawyer to represent Xavier in Marseilles, and that she should arrange to fly to Marseilles to coordinate his defence as soon as possible. Farah was a bit confused by the major's comments regarding Xavier's defence, but the situation was made clearer to her when the major advised her that he had been alerted by the Marseilles detectives on the case that Xavier would be charged with sexual assault, probably within the next few days. The major then offered to Farah that he was more than willing to inform Xavier's parents, but Farah told him that she would look after that, just as soon as she was off the phone with him.

THOMAS SUTTON AND Mirabel Soliano, Xavier's parents, were both on the line when Farah explained to them the troubling and disturbing news, and after she had finished speaking, they very quickly let her know that they shared her position, that there must have been a setup orchestrated by someone or some entity that had something to gain by harming Xavier. They knew their son, just like Farah knew her husband, and they were certain that he was not capable of doing anything like what was alleged. Farah was heartened by Thomas and Mirabel's pledge to do whatever it took, and to spend whatever was required, to free him from his terrible situation and get him back home as soon as possible. Thomas assured Farah that he would arrange for the best legal representation available in Marseilles, and that he would make all the arrangements for them to fly to Marseilles at the earliest available time.

Thomas and Mirabel knew that Farah would be feeling very lonely and vulnerable as she tried to deal with the terrible news coming out of Marseilles. When Farah had decided to marry Xavier, against her father's wishes, she had effectively been disowned by him, and that meant that her mother and her siblings had to abide by this verdict as well. Thomas and Mirabel knew that Farah would need their support now more than ever.

CHAPTER 3

Xavier thought about his upcoming 2019 Christmas break, which he intended to spend with his family in Kuala Lumpur, as he stood with some of his fellow pilots and watched the Prime Minister of Malaysia and the Crown Prince of the local state royalty cut the ceremonial ribbon, opening the new port complex on the east coast of the state. The month was December, which meant that the businessman behind the port project, Hassan Ahmad, was delivering on his promise to the government that the port would be ready by the end of 2019. Hassan was one of Malaysia's "chosen ones," the type of businessman who, through close connections with the state governments, the state royalties, and the federal government, was often chosen to construct the government's massive infrastructure projects, or to be granted lucrative concessions to operate them. These businessmen became fabulously wealthy due to the government's largess, but while they lined their pockets, the government ended up overpaying substantially for the work that was done, and for the services that were provided. It was impossible for the vested interests within the government, and for the entitled ones within the royal families, as well as the companies undertaking the projects, to amass the huge amounts of money that they expected from the projects, without the government closing a blind eye to the costs.

The airbase where Xavier was stationed was not far from the new port facilities, and the government had decided that it would be fitting for the country's air force, as well as its navy, to be represented at the opening ceremonies. The government had always been very effective in marketing their extravagant infrastructure projects, so that it looked as if they were doing something for the people that elected them. The Malaysian population, however, did not see any of the benefits that accrued from these huge investments, as those benefits were reserved for the chosen ones, such as Hassan Ahmad.

Xavier was quite bored, standing around with some of his fellow pilots, waiting for the dinner to commence, when he noticed a young woman amongst a small crowd of ladies, all of whom were wearing beautiful Malay baju kurung outfits. Xavier had always admired the look of the traditional Malay dress on the Malay women, but today he was especially impressed with the young woman in the teal blue ensemble.

As everyone made their way to their assigned tables, Xavier kept his eyes open for the young woman in teal, and he was pleasantly surprised when he saw that she was seated just one table over from his. Xavier did not really pay much attention to the multiple dishes that were served, or to the conversations going on at his table, as he was preoccupied with trying to catch the eye of his lovely target. Xavier's persistence eventually paid off, as he found himself staring directly into her amazing large, brown eyes on a few occasions, and after making contact, he convinced himself that she was looking at him as much as he

was looking at her. There were other little signs of acknowledge-
ment that Xavier detected, including a few little smiles over
the duration of the meal, but the dinner was finishing, and he
didn't know how to find a way, or enough courage, to meet this
amazing young woman.

Xavier was making his way out of the dining area, feeling as
if a wonderful opportunity was going to pass him by, when a
young Malay man tapped him on the shoulder. He introduced
himself as Reza Hassan, and then he asked Xavier if he would
like to join him and some of this family members for a coffee at
the new coffee bar that had just opened in the complex. Xavier
did not know who this Reza was, but nothing required him back
at the base early, so he accepted his invitation and followed him
along the boardwalk to the trendy new coffee bar. Xavier asked
Reza why he had invited him, and he quickly learned that it was
his sister, Farah, that had asked him to extend the invitation.

When they arrived at the seating section, Xavier couldn't
believe his good fortune. Reza took him directly to the lovely
young lady in teal and introduced her as his sister, Farah. Xavier
softly shook her tender hand, without taking his eyes from hers,
for what he thought must have seemed like a long time for the
others at the table, and then he finally settled into an available seat
across from her. As coffees were enjoyed and the conversation
flowed, Xavier soon realized that he was sitting with the children
of the businessman Hassan Ahmad, and that the woman he was
now certain he wanted to marry was his youngest daughter.

After Xavier had returned to his base that evening, he sat on
the edge of his bed, feeling like he had been blessed with one
of those life altering opportunities. He took one final look at
Farah's phone number, which he had safely stored in his phone,
before turning out his bedside lamp.

THE NEXT DAY, he and his fellow pilot Lt. Colonel Lim were called into the base commander's office, where they were advised that they had been selected as the test pilots on the air force's technical committee. The commander's first order of business was to inform the pilots that the Ministry of Defence and the Ministry of Finance had finally approved the air force's budget for the purchase of new fighter jets. The technical committee that they were being appointed to was charged with reviewing the two jet options that had been shortlisted—the F35 Jet from the USA, and the Vitesse Jet from the French supplier, Delorme Aviation. He made it very clear to them that their recommendations would be critical in determining which jet was recommended to the ministries, for their final approval, and that they should view their work as being in the national interest. The commanding officer did not enlighten the pilots as to the existence of the commercial committee, which dealt with the financial considerations for the contract, as those activities were primarily handled by the Ministry of Finance. The final instruction given by the commanding officer was for the pilots to be ready to travel on very short notice, with the first trip to South Carolina to test the F35, and the second trip to Marseilles, France to test the Vitesse. With respect to the actual travel dates, he advised them that the dates were presently being finalized with the vendors, but that they should be prepared to travel as early as January.

Xavier was more than thrilled that he had been chosen for the technical committee, and he couldn't stop thinking about what a wonderful opportunity he had been given. His good news must have given him the dose of courage that he needed to recall the special number he had stored in his phone, and then to push the call button to connect with Farah Hassan, whom he had been thinking about nonstop since he met her at the port opening event the night before.

Farah was getting caught up on some reports at work when her phone buzzed, and when she heard Xavier identify himself, she had no difficulty putting her work aside so that she could focus on her conversation with him. She did not tell him that she had been waiting anxiously for him to call, but she did let him know how happy she was that he had called. Xavier felt a bit awkward jumping right into his air force business, but he wanted her to know about his upcoming trips, and how excited he was to be on the air force's technical committee. Farah informed Xavier that she was not very familiar with military or air force matters, but she did congratulate him on his appointment, and she offered the comment that he must be a very accomplished pilot to be given such an honour.

Although this was their first real conversation, they both seemed very comfortable sharing bits of information about themselves, including the somewhat awkward revelations that they were both in relationships with other people. Xavier felt more than a little jealous when Farah admitted that she was in an intimate relationship, but he was heartened by her comment that she did not see any long-term prospects with her boyfriend.

Farah, on her end, felt she was on more even footing once Xavier revealed that he had been seeing someone for the past few months, but that their prospects for the future were quite low. Xavier knew that he would be spending the weekend at the beach with his girlfriend Alexa, and he knew that she would be a good test for him to see how he felt about Farah.

Xavier wasn't the only one who had big weekend plans, as Farah and her boyfriend would be celebrating their six-month anniversary. Both Xavier and Farah committed to staying in touch on the phone over the next few weeks, and they agreed to meet for lunch when Xavier arrived in Kuala Lumpur for his holiday break.

XAVIER AND LIM were catching some good sun as they paddled their surf boards into the mild waves outside their holiday cabins. When they looked back at the beach, they could see their partners looking very impressive in their colourful bathing suits as they slowly strolled the secluded beach. As they settled into some calm water before the next batch of waves arrived, Xavier told Lim that he had met the girl of his dreams at the port opening, that her name was Farah, and that he couldn't get her out of his mind. Lim, who always had his sense of humour, suggested that he take a good look at who was waiting for him at the cabin, if he needed something to get his mind off her. Xavier acknowledged to Lim that Alexa, his British architect friend, was a wonderful woman in many respects, but that he was looking for a lot more in the person he would want to marry, and that he felt that Farah could be the one. Lim informed Xavier, while trying to keep a straight face, that if his wife was not here then he would be happy to take the architect off his hands. Not to be outdone by his senior flying partner, Xavier jokingly said that he would gladly take Lim's wife in return.

As Xavier sat on the beach that evening with Alexa after another amazing day, he thought that this might be one of the last times they would spend together. Regardless, he was going to enjoy it for as long as he could before his pursuit of Farah continued.

FARAH HAD MADE it clear to her boyfriend Amin that she did not want to marry him, but he did not seem to be deterred, and in fact he became increasingly attentive to her ever since she had advised him of her decision. Despite her decision to not commit to a long-term relationship with Amin, Farah welcomed the additional intimate time that he spent with her.

Farah had initially been very shy regarding sexual relations, but her times with Amin had enabled her to experience the most extreme levels of pleasure. She became very accommodating to him, and she willingly embraced all his requests. Unfortunately for Farah, she soon learned from some of her friends that he was extending the same pleasures to two other young ladies as well. Once she had learned that Amin was not exclusive to her, she decided to break it off with him when he least expected it. As their six-month anniversary approached, she decided that it was an ideal time to exact some bittersweet revenge.

Farah was spending an extra long time in the shower, as she was nervous about giving Amin the news that their relationship was over, though they had fully satisfied each other the night before, and there was no better time to surprise him with the news.

Amin reacted poorly, as Farah had predicted he would, but she had not anticipated being called some of the vile names that he directed at her. She didn't know if Amin had spoken to her father about his intentions to marry her, or if he would be complaining to him about her leaving him, but she had made her decision to move on, and she was now ready to discover what could happen with Xavier.

XAVIER COULD NOT remember the last time he was so nervous, as he sat in the lobby of the Concorde hotel waiting for Farah to arrive for their long anticipated, in-person meeting. Farah had advised Xavier that she would be driving a silver Mini, and when he saw her vehicle entering the hotel driveway, he quickly made his way to the glass sliding doors. Farah was dressed in light-coloured, linen pants with a matching jacket, and Xavier thought that she looked even more amazing than she had on the evening when he had first met her.

She gave Xavier the most wonderful smile and a soft hand-shake before they made their way to a quiet table at the back of the restaurant. Xavier very politely asked the waiter to give them a few minutes, since neither of them had even looked at the menu— they had been more interested in looking at each other, and on exchanging some best wishes for the Christmas holiday season.

Xavier's nature was to be very engaging, but he sensed that Farah was considerably more guarded, and he took a mental note that he would need to be respectful of that quality, and to also be mindful of the fact that she did not engage in idle chatter. It was no surprise that they did not discuss anything regarding their personal relationships, as these were delicate matters best kept to themselves for now.

Farah advised Xavier that she was leaving with her family the next day, to spend the holiday break at their country home, and that she would be away for the rest of his stay in Kuala Lumpur. Xavier had previously made Farah aware of his pending trips to South Carolina and Marseilles, so he decided to take this opportunity to let her know that his work on the air force com-mittee was going to keep him quite busy for the first few months of the new year. Their first face to face meeting since meeting at the port opening ceremony was not awkward in anyway – in fact they were both very comfortable, and their body language – most specifically their eye contacts - demonstrated a strong attraction to one another.

Xavier and Farah were both very happy as they walked out to

the front of the hotel and waited for the valet to retrieve her car. When Xavier gently closed her car door, he thought of leaning in and giving her a small peck on the cheek, but instead he told her that he would be calling her, and he also warned her that she might find him to be a pest before too long.

Farah had a satisfied smile on her face when she gave Xavier a little wave through her car window, and then she prepared to merge into the busy Kuala Lumpur traffic.

XAVIER AND LIM found themselves spending the middle part of January on the east coast of the United States for the first of their fighter jet technical evaluation visits. They unpacked in the officer quarters that had been assigned to them at the US military base in Beaufort, South Carolina, and reflected on the crazy route they had to take to get there. It had involved a flight from Kuala Lumpur to London, followed by another flight to Atlanta, Georgia, and then a three-hour drive in their rental car to Beaufort.

They realized that the long route that they had taken was well worth the time after they got up in their F35 fighter jets. This latest generation of fighter aircraft had been developed jointly by the USA and its NATO partners, and it had become the preferred choice of many air forces around the world. As Xavier and Lim engaged in the predetermined test flight maneuvers that took them along the eastern coast of South Carolina and out over the Atlantic, they experienced superior handling and performance capabilities that far exceeded even their own lofty expectations. The American naval pilots, who were flying alongside the Malaysians, advised them that even within their own extensive arsenal of fighter aircraft, the F35 was considered the "dream machine."

Xavier and Lim also got the opportunity, during their time at Beaufort, to spend some time with two members of the US Navy's Top Gun program, that was recognized worldwide as being the pinnacle of achievement for jet fighter pilots. Some of the stories and experiences that they shared with Xavier just reinforced his commitment and his passion to becoming the best fighter pilot the Royal Malaysian Air Force had ever seen. The two Top Gun pilots had been engaged in America's ongoing conflicts in the Middle East, and they were able to share with the Malaysians just how intense a war environment was. Xavier did not aspire to be involved in any war, or to have to engage any of the powerful weapon systems on the advanced fighter jets, but he certainly felt his adrenaline rise when he listened to the Top Gun pilots describe their experiences.

Lim commented to Xavier, during the last leg of their return flights from Atlanta, that he wondered whether the people in charge would be supporting the F35 or the Vitesse. Xavier was a little confused, and he told Lim that it would be difficult to see how anyone could possibly recommend, let alone approve, the purchase of any aircraft other than the F35. Lim, who had considerably more experience than Xavier in terms of flying, and who had also been exposed to the military's vendor selection process, could see that Xavier was very naïve, and that he did not understand the intrusion of politics and their vested interests into large government purchases. He could see that naïveté from the perplexed look on Xavier's face when he told him that they would get a better idea of where things stood once they had completed their test flights in the French Vitesse jets. Xavier advised Lim that he had done some research on the Vitesse, and from what he could determine, it did not provide much of an upgrade from the air force's existing Russian-made

Mig jets. Lim smiled and told Xavier that the pilots would not be the ones making the decisions, as the key decisions were always made by the politicians, and that they had to satisfy their vested interests, not the air force's interests. Xavier understood what Lim was saying, but he still maintained that it would be difficult to overlook the superiority of the F35.

Xavier had kept in touch with Farah while he was in South Carolina, and during their phone calls he was able to learn a little more about her Harvard days and her important work at the Central Bank of Malaysia, but he noted that she did not offer many insights into her own family. Xavier knew that her father was well known as a businessman who owed his success primarily to his close government relationships, but he had learned very little from Farah about her mother or about her many siblings. Farah was very forthcoming with respect to her relationship status when she happily informed Xavier that she was finally done with her boyfriend. Farah did not mention to Xavier that she would likely face some stern opposition to her dumping of Amin, nor did she mention that the bulk of that opposition would likely come from her father. Xavier made sure that she knew that he was most appreciative of her decision to end her relationship. He followed up with an invitation to a dinner at his parent's home, which his mother was organizing for him upon his return from the United States. Farah agreed to come.

Xavier had been trying to figure out how he could acceler-ate his courtship of Farah, so he was more than pleased when he was informed by his commanding officer, that both he and Lim would be given extended leave before their evaluation trip to Marseilles.

FARAH NODDED TO the security guard at the gates, before driving her Mini up to the Sutton's house, located in the exclusive Kenny Hills area of Kuala Lumpur. When Xavier had invited Farah to meet his family at the celebratory dinner, he had assured her that there would be fish and vegetarian dishes that would comply with her Muslim dietary restrictions.

Xavier's mother, Mirabel Soliano, was the first to greet Farah, and she welcomed her with a very warm embrace and a gentle kiss on both cheeks.

Mirabel was a very attractive lady of Eurasian descent, and when Farah looked at her, she could see very clearly who Xavier got his wonderful skin tones from.

Thomas Sutton, who did not have that wonderful olive skin, was a traditionally handsome man, who Farah discovered over the course of the dinner, was also a kind man and a humble man. She had done her homework on the Suttons, and she had learned that the Sutton Group was a multi-billion-dollar frozen baked goods company, whose roots were in Canada, and that they had operations in most parts of the world. When she discovered how affluent the Suttons were, she was enormously impressed with Xavier, as he had not mentioned anything about that aspect of his family to her. All that he had told her was that his father was from Canada, and that he had come to Malaysia to work for the family business, and that his mother's family was involved in the food supermarket business. Farah was not impressed with money or all the garish displays of wealth that had become all too prevalent in Malaysia, including within her own family.

Farah's father, Hassan Ahmad, unlike Thomas Sutton, liked to show off his possessions, which included a private jet, a large yacht, and multiple homes in Malaysia and abroad. Even more disturbing than his tasteless displays of wealth was the arrogance that he displayed in the way in which he treated people, including those within his own family. He had handpicked his daughters' husbands, most of whom worked either directly or indirectly for him. His own beautiful wife, Raja Soraya, had been procured through a negotiation between himself and her father. His choice of Amin for his youngest daughter was based on a commitment he'd made to Amin's father, who was a valued business associate, and one of the "chosen ones." He had made this commitment to Amin's father, despite warnings from his own son Reza that Amin had a reputation for being a womanizer, and that he was seeing two other women in addition to Farah. Hassan had laughed when Reza made him aware of these facts about Farah's boyfriend, and then he told him that Farah would have to learn how to keep him at home. He clearly did not think that the women in his family were worthy of having an opinion on who their mates would be. The comfortable and respectful world of the Suttons was, fortunately, a far cry from the tyrannical and chauvinistic world that was ruled by Hassan Ahmad.

CHAPTER 4

bbas and Asad Khalil were sitting around their circular conference room table talking to Robert Khoury, one of their senior military sales agents, about how the year 2020 was shaping up, while they admired the many super yachts that were anchored in the Monte Carlo main harbour. They could see their own super yacht, as they looked out through the huge, floor-to-ceiling windows; it was anchored further offshore, with some of the other larger vessels. The brothers made sure to let Robert know that the chartering of their yacht had brought them in more money than all his military sales had over the past two years. This was the month of February, so it was quite rare to see so many large yachts in Monte Carlo during the off season, but the world was awash with billionaires from Russia and the United States, to name just a few of the countries that were represented in the harbour, and there were only so many places to park their huge yachts.

Robert Khoury was not just one of the Khalil's sales agents, he was one of their closest friends from their early days growing up in Lebanon. The Khourys and the Khalils were farming families from the rich agricultural area of Lebanon known as the Bekaa Valley, and both families had sufficient means to send their children to the better private schools located in Beirut. Under the supervision of the lax priests at the school they attended, Robert and the Khalils were able to explore their curiosities with the darker sides of Lebanese life. They started out as runners and errand boys for some of the local street gangs, which eventually led them to their employment with one of the leading arms merchants in the area. As the years progressed, the Khalils gained the confidence of their boss through their street smarts and willingness to deliver the required messages of violence when required. Robert also had skills that were linked to his handsome looks, which the arms merchant used to his advantage when he needed to secure the services of suitable young ladies to help convince a reluctant customer. The details surrounding the death of the arms merchant were very murky, but what was clear after his death was that the Khalil brothers had taken control of the company, and that Robert Khoury was one of their sales agents. As the brothers often reminded Robert, he would be sitting with them if he hadn't devoted so much of his time to the pursuit and conquest of pretty women.

Abbas reminded Robert that they were still very upset with the loss of the Moroccan tank contract, which he had previously assured them would be a guaranteed sale. Robert, who still felt the personal sting from losing that contract, reminded Abbas that the military chief in Morocco had received a higher percentage from the South African supplier, and that neither he nor Asad would match the offer. Robert must have felt it was necessary to emphasize that point, as he had been repeatedly accused by the brothers of losing the contract because he got caught sleeping with the Moroccan general's daughter. Having made his point to Robert regarding his past failures, Asad asked him to explain where everything presently stood, with respect to the Malaysian fighter jet contract. Robert advised him that he had reached agreements with individuals in both the finance ministry and the defence ministry, with respect to what they would deliver, and what percentage they would receive for their participation. He then informed the brothers, who probably already knew from their own back channels, that the Malaysian air force's technical committee had completed their visit to test the F35 in South Carolina, and that they were working on travel dates to test the Delorme Vitesse jets. Robert understood just as much as his bosses did that the technical committee was the critical piece in ensuring that the Malaysians chose the French jets. Their recommendations could destroy all his development work, and all the financial arrangements he had put in place, if they recommended the American jets over the French ones, and if the air force superiors supported their recommendation.

Abbas, who was the more forceful of the brothers, made it very clear to Robert that he had to do whatever it took to make sure that the technical committee recommended the Delorme jets, as they would not continue to finance his failed efforts.

Robert understood just how serious Abbas was, friendship or no friendship, and he pledged to deliver the Malaysian jet contract award to him. He then excused himself, so that he could attend the 2020 edition of the Malaysia World Fashion Show, which was being held in the convention hall just adjacent to their offices. It was no coincidence that the Khalils' holding company was the title sponsor of the event.

As Robert was leaving the room, Abbas told him that he knew that he had his magical ways with women, but that he had better keep it in his pants until the Malaysian deal was in the bank. Robert told himself, as he was leaving the office, that he had to be prepared to go beyond what was normally required to influence a decision, regardless of how dangerous, or how distasteful it may be, to ensure that the Malaysian air force chose the Delorme Aviation jets.

ROBERT COMMENTED TO the two middle aged Malaysian ladies sitting on either side of him just how lovely the Malay models looked in the traditional Malay outfits that they were modelling. The ladies on his sides were the wives of his partners from the Malaysian ministries of finance and defence, and he was making sure that they had nothing but nice things to say to their husbands when they got home. Dinners at fine restaurants, shopping at designer boutiques, and private city tours were just some of the costs of dealing with corrupt government officials that military sales agents accepted as the cost of doing business. Robert's problem was that there was too much money going toward those costs, and not enough coming back to justify the investment. The larger the contract was, the larger the investment that was required of the sales agents, and those investments could go on for two or three years during the contract development process, before a sale was even made. Although the wives of the Malaysian ministry officials appeared to be very distant and unaware of their husbands' greed, they were in many ways the driving forces behind the corrupt actions that took place. They made sure that their husbands knew that they expected to have all the luxuries and other benefits accrued by the most ambitious government officials.

Robert did not spend a lot of time thinking about the financial aspects of what he did, aside from his own considerable compensations, but he always had time for a pretty woman, and he had spotted one across the room that he thought was looking very enticing in her traditional Malay outfit. As the Khalils were the sponsors of the event, Robert was able to gain access to the attendees' names and their seat assignments. He easily found out that the lady who had caught his eye was Raja Noor, and after asking one of the Malay organizers a few questions, he learned that she was twice divorced, that she had considerable personal wealth, and that she was presently single. Robert could see that she was quite a bit older than he was, but something about her intrigued him.

Robert's Malaysian wives were spending their last evening in Monte Carlo with some of their Malaysian friends, so Robert knew that he was free to pursue his Malaysian divorcée. As the attendees were enjoying the offerings from the extensive display of finger foods and fresh fruit that had been set up in the glass-walled foyer, Robert very quietly made his way to where Raja Noor was standing, and then he introduced himself to her as someone representing the sponsoring company.

Robert was a tall man, and he was extremely handsome, and as Raja Noor looked up at him, she had a look of amazement on her face, as if she was trying to figure out why this great-looking guy had introduced himself to her, and why he was asking her about her experiences in Monte Carlo. Whether it was Robert's looks or his overall charm, Raja Noor agreed to join him for dinner that evening. She certainly did not represent the norm with respect to how Malaysian women conducted themselves in personal matters, and in fact her very cavalier approach to men and relationships had earned her somewhat of an unenviable reputation in some circles of Malaysian society. In Raja Noor's case, she had benefited very handsomely from a financial perspective, through her two divorces, and this seemed to have emboldened her to test the limits of what was acceptable to Malaysian society. In many ways, she was snubbing her nose at them.

As Robert and Raja Noor drove in the chauffeured vehicle that he had picked her up with, she enjoyed the view of the wonderful yachts docked in the main port. They stopped at a point on the harbour where a launch was waiting to take them out to sea.

Raja Noor looked over at Robert, trying to hold her hair from blowing in her face, and asked him where they were going. He simply replied that they would be there soon.

When the launch stopped at one of the larger yachts anchored offshore, and a uniformed staff member escorted her onto the main deck of the yacht, Raja Noor felt like she was in a world that she was not familiar with. Robert Khoury had used this impressive vessel for similar purposes in the past, when it was not being chartered out by its owners, the Khalils, and he always felt that he had great success when he used it. Robert had always indicated to his bosses that he needed the yacht for business reasons, as he knew that they would never approve of his using the yacht to serve his personal desires.

After a wonderful meal and a few bottles of the finest French wines, courtesy of the Khalils, Raja Noor found herself looking over at her handsome young friend, lounging in the ship's hot tub, while he enjoyed his Cuban cigar. Robert had made sure that she was able to get a quick glimpse of him as he entered the hot tub, as he was confident that she would be impressed.

Raja Noor was totally taken in by all of Robert's charms, which included his well rehearsed "rags to riches" story, which took him from the tough streets of Beirut through all the challenges that he had to overcome along the way, to now being able to enjoy himself on a super yacht anchored in Monte Carlo. She knew that he was likely using her to satisfy his curiosities about older women, but she didn't care, as she had curiosities of her own which she intended to satisfy. Raja Noor, like many others before her, was very willingly brought under the control of a very wicked, very convincing womanizer.

Robert knew that he would be spending a lot of time in Kuala Lumpur over the next few years, as part of the process of working the network that he had set up to secure the Air Force jet contract, so having someone to spend time with while he was there was a welcome development. Robert neglected to mention to Raja Noor that if he had to make comments and promises to her that he didn't really mean, he would be comfortable doing so.

As the launch ferried them back to shore in the morning, the smiles on both of their faces suggested that neither of them had any complaints about how the evening had gone. The chauffeured vehicle arrived at the front of Raja Noor's hotel, but before she got out, Raja Noor turned to Robert, and she asked if he might like to join her for lunch in her suite, as her flight did not leave until ten o'clock at night. Robert gave Raja Noor a kiss and told her that he would be at her hotel suite door at two o'clock.

They had just finished their lunch when Raja Noor excused herself and went to the bedroom in the suite, while Robert made his way to the expansive balcony to digest with one of his Cuban cigars. When Robert returned, after finishing his cigar, he found that his host had spread out the bedspread and pillows from the bedroom in the middle of the living room. As he watched Raja Noor slowly walking towards the temporary bed she had established, he could see from the natural way that she presented herself, and from the way that everything moved, that she was different from the women he was used to, but his mind took him to his recent experiences on the yacht, and he quickly forgot about age.

Robert was giving Raja Noor a gentle massage when he advised her that he would be in Malaysia, on and off, over the next year or so, as he was working on an important project. She was very immersed in the wonderful handiwork of her lunch companion, but she made sure that he knew that he did not need to worry about hotel accommodations, when she informed him that she had more than enough room at her penthouse apartment in Kuala Lumpur. Raja Noor was clearly under the control of her younger, Lebanese paramour, and she had successfully demonstrated to him that she wanted to continue enjoying his company, both in Monte Carlo and in Malaysia.

CHAPTER 5

avier was looking forward to meeting some of Farah's family, and he was pleasantly surprised to see a few familiar faces as he entered the hospital suite, where one of her sisters was receiving family members who had come to congratulate her on the birth of her daughter. The second oldest of Farah's three sisters, who had just given birth to her second child, sat up in her bed, and she told Xavier and Farah that she was so pleased to see the handsome pilot again.

When Xavier heard this, he started to think that maybe he would be accepted by Farah's family. Farah had made him aware of the fact that many in her family, like many of the Malays, didn't really like the western people who came to Malaysia to exploit the financial opportunities that existed, and they especially despised those who thought they could seduce their precious women. Farah had been present on a few occasions when her father spoke to her sisters about staying clear of any "mat saleh," as the white men were called in Malaysia, as he said that all that they wanted was a quick fling. Farah wasn't the only one in her family that knew that white men were not exclusive to that group, but Hassan Ahmad had blinders on when it came to foreigners.

Farah and Xavier were walking to the door after a nice long visit with her sister, when they were surprised to see Hassan Ahmad and his lovely wife Raja Soraya coming into the suite.

Xavier stood back and watched as Farah gracefully moved to take her father's hand, followed by her mother's, in the respectful way of greeting your parents, before she introduced them to him, and then he and Farah waited for what would come next.

It didn't take long before Hassan began his barrage of questions for Xavier, which he directed at him as if he was interviewing a candidate for a job. His line of questioning clearly revealed his intentions of trying to determine who he was and what he did, but most importantly, what was going on between him and his youngest daughter? He started in with,

"Xavier, how do you like our country?"

Xavier was surprised and a bit offended by the question.

"Since I was born here and I have lived here my whole life, I like it very much."

Hassan looked to be a little taken back by Xavier's response.

"I am sorry, I just assumed that you were a foreigner. We Muslims tend to be very protective, and I hope you understand that."

Xavier clearly saw what he was getting at.

"No apologies necessary. And I want to compliment both you and your wife on your amazing daughter Farah."

Hassan, realizing that Xavier was very capable of holding his own, must have felt the need to deliver a clear message.

"I assume you know that Farah is committed to the son of one of our close family friends."

Xavier was now starting to see that Farah's father did not care if his comments offended anyone.

"No, I wasn't aware of that, but I am sure Farah will let me know if it is a matter that I need to be concerned about."

Farah couldn't tell from her father's comments if Amin had spoken to him or not, but it didn't seem to matter. Her father was very disrespectful to Xavier.

As Xavier was engaged in the verbal duel with Hassan, he also found himself drawn to Farah's mother, not because she was an attractive woman, but because she had what Xavier later told Farah was a look of sad resignation on her face. Xavier could clearly see that Farah got her beauty from her mother, but he could also see that her mother didn't have her wonderful radiance, and in fact, Xavier thought that with her sad expression she looked like a beautiful princess who hadn't gotten her dashing prince.

Xavier could sense that Farah had reached her limit with the inquisition her father was staging, as she politely said that they had to get to another engagement. What Farah did next, brought a few tears to Xavier's eyes. She went to her mother and warmly embraced her with both arms, and then she kissed her so lovingly on her cheek.

When they got out into the hospital hallway, Xavier turned to Farah and told her that he could see very clearly that she loved her mother very much. They didn't talk much about Farah's father and his relentless questioning, but Farah did enlighten Xavier on the connection between her ex-boyfriend and her father.

Xavier had one more day and one more night with Farah before he returned to the airbase, and he would be back at her place following dinner, as he would be having dinner with his family, and some of his mother's siblings.

Farah told Xavier that she had just decided that she was going to go see her mother, and to get some sound motherly advice on marriage.

Raja Soraya was a cousin of the Sultan of one of the western states in Malaysia, and she had grown up in a family that was very insistent upon following both Muslim and royal traditions. Unfortunately for her, one of those traditions was arranged marriages, and in her case that meant her marriage to Hassan Ahmad, a man that she neither knew nor loved. Raja Soraya's father, although being a member of the state royalty, did not enjoy the same financial benefits accrued by the Sultan and his immediate family members, so he had to make decisions which often involved compromises, to ensure that his daughters were able to enjoy the type of privileged life that he envisioned for them. There was a strong misconception that all the royals in Malaysia were rich and that they all lived in palaces, but nothing could be further from the truth. In fact, there were only small numbers from each of the nine royal families in Malaysia that lived the lavish lifestyle that everyone assumed royals enjoyed. For the most part, royals worked in society and held down positions and ranks in the same way that other Malaysians did. The difference was that they were afforded a level of respect, due to the titles in front of their names. But respect did not buy them palaces or lavish lifestyles.

Hassan Ahmad did not have to resort to finding financially capable spouses for his daughters, as he was more than capable and willing to look after their financial needs, but he arranged marriages for his daughters so that he could control every aspect of their lives. Just as his own wife had no say in him becoming her husband, Hassan made sure that his daughters, including Farah, had very little to say in who their spouses would be. Fortunately for some of Farah's sisters, they had found boyfriends that met with their father's approval, but that was not going to be the case with Farah and her Malaysian pilot.

FARAH AND HER mother decided to sit out in the beautiful back gardens of the family home to enjoy their tea and what turned out to be a very frank and hurtful discussion.

"Farah, your father is furious that you are spending time with a non-Muslim, and he asked me to inform you that he fully expects you to marry Amin."

Farah looked at her mother with intensity in her eyes.

"You might like to know that Amin was sleeping with two other women while he was with me, and I could not accept that."

Raja Soraya did not seem to be moved by Farah's revelation.

"I have endured many humiliations in my marriage, and I can assure you that it involved considerably more than two women. Sometimes that is what is required."

Farah pleaded with her mother.

"I am sorry that you have had to put up with all of that, but that is why you should understand my situation and why I cannot accept what I am being asked to do. And I won't"

Raja Soraya then made herself very clear.

"I sympathize with you Farah, but I cannot go against your father's wishes, and you better be prepared because all of your sisters and your brother will be forced to hold that same position."

THAT LAST COMMENT from her mother was like a blow to Farah's heart. The only important ally that she could have counted on from within her family would have been her mother.

The only indication of support for Farah coming from within

her family was a phone call she received later that day, from her older brother Reza, who told her that he had warned their father about Amin's womanizing ways, and that he was going to see if he could get their father to loosen up his strict position on marriage. Farah was thankful for Reza's call, but Reza worked for their father, and she knew that since he was his heir apparent, he was unlikely to do anything to jeopardize that position.

EVERYONE IN THE Sutton house was more than a little surprised when Xavier's possessive, teen aged sister Aldia shared her thoughts, that she felt Xavier's plan to ask Farah to marry him was a good one. Xavier could not have thought of a more unlikely person to support his intentions to marry, but Farah had obviously had a very important and helpful impact on his younger sister. Thomas and Mirabel both expressed how much they adored Farah, and how she seemed so right for Xavier, but they made him aware of the challenges, including the decision he would have to make to convert to Islam. Xavier told his parents that he had given it some thought, and that during the few days at the airbase, before starting his Christmas break, he had spoken with a fellow Malay pilot. They had discussed what was involved in becoming a Muslim. Xavier wanted his family to know that he had been very ignorant about Islam and what was involved in being a Muslim, and that the main reason for that was due to the biased reporting on Islam in the Western press that, unfortunately, influenced so many people. He explained to his family that he could not see his future life without Farah in it, and he was fully prepared to convert to a religion that he believed to be thoughtful and peaceful.

There was not a lot of prejudice, or racism, or any other negative beliefs within the Sutton family, and Thomas made it very clear to Xavier that if he decided to convert to Islam, and to marry Farah, he could count on their full and genuine support.

XAVIER'S LAST NIGHT at Farah's townhouse before returning to work was the most important day in his short life. He got down on one knee and formally asked Farah to marry him. Farah did not keep him on his knee for long before giving him her definitive yes, after which they warmly embraced each other, and Farah gave him a meaningful hug, and the type of kiss that he would not soon forget. They had not wasted a lot of time in reaching a decision that they were meant to be together, and they had done so with their mutual agreement to remain celibate until after they were married.

They discussed the good news coming out of the Sutton house, and the disappointing news coming out of the Hassan house, but they were both fully committed to the position that what mattered most to them was that they were going to be getting married. As Xavier took Farah in his arms, he let her know that he would do anything for her, and that his family would also be there for her. As she whispered her thank you in his ear, he told her that she would never be alone to face the tough struggles that may be ahead of them. It was another night of abstinence, but it was a wonderful night, knowing that their future together was in front of them.

Xavier's ride arrived outside her driveway gate, and he kissed Farah very passionately. As Xavier was walking down the driveway, she asked him to please be careful in those powerful jets.

XAVIER WAS JUST getting settled into his hotel room in Marseille when his hotel room phone rang. It was Lim, who wanted to know his opinion on the accommodations that Delorme had arranged for them. Xavier acknowledged to Lim that the room was quite an upgrade from the officer quarters in South Carolina, but that he was more focused on getting up in the Vitesse jet and testing it out than he was on how luxurious his hotel room was. Fortunately for Xavier, the flight routes for the test maneuvers took them over the city of Marseilles and along the southern coast before heading out over the Mediterranean. This enabled him to see the full majesty of the city of Marseilles, with all its ports filled with every kind of sea vessel, as well as the wonderful hillsides and landscapes that surrounded the city. Xavier thought to himself, as he was flying over the city, that Delorme Aviation had probably chosen this flight route so that it would put the test pilots in a better mood, which would then influence them to see the Vitesse in a more favourable light. He knew that was nonsense, but he said to himself that the mind works in funny ways when one is faced with uncertain situations.

Xavier enjoyed the experience he had in the Vitesse jet, but it wasn't like the F35, and he knew from the moment that he initiated some of the aerial maneuvers that his recommendation to the technical committee would be in favour of the F35.

Just as the Americans had made two of the Top Gun pilots available to them in South Carolina, Delorme made sure that two of the Egyptian pilots presently training with the French air force were on hand for their flight trials. Unlike the interesting commentaries on wartime conditions for a fighter pilot that the Top Gun pilots shared with Xavier and Lim, the Egyptians seemed to be following a well rehearsed script put together by Delorme on the wonderful benefits of the Vitesse jets. Xavier and Lim did not have any problem with the Egyptians playing the roles they were asked to play, as they knew full well how the F35 and the Vitesse stacked up against each other.

Xavier gave Lim a nudge, as he could see that he was nodding off in his comfortable airline seat, and he asked him how the Vitesse compared to the F35 for him. Lim, who always seemed to be laid back, told Xavier that it was as obvious to him, as it would be to any pilot, that the F35 was in a league of its own, and that if he was buying, he would take the F35. Xavier was happy to hear Lim confirm what he thought about the jets, and then he offered the comment to Lim that their recommendations to the technical committee were going to be very straightforward. Lim, however, suggested that they wait a few weeks before they submitted their formal recommendations, as there may be other factors that they would want to consider. Xavier knew that there was corruption in the military, just like there was in every other ministry, but he didn't see how anyone, corrupt or not, could justify the purchase of the French jets. Lim then let Xavier in on something that he had been advised of just prior to their trip to Marseilles. He had been informed that his name had been advanced for promotion to the full rank of colonel. Lim informed Xavier that this was remarkable since his eligibility for advancement to full colonel was still two years away. Why did Xavier think that they were advancing Lim so quickly? Lim knew full well that pilots and other enlisted men were usually enticed with offers like the rank advancement that he was being offered, or with training opportunities with foreign air forces like Xavier had been offered, but these were tough decisions that had to be made as an individual, not as a member of the air force.

Xavier congratulated him on the advancement news, but he told Lim that he didn't see how his promotion advancement had anything to do with the jet contract.

Lim, who was adjusting his business class seat to the lie flat position, looked over at Xavier, and told him that they should both just wait and see what transpired over the next few weeks. Realizing that he wasn't going to get any more out of Lim, Xavier put his seat to lie flat, and joined him in trying to sleep for the remaining six hours of the flight to Kuala Lumpur.

ONCE XAVIER ARRIVED back in Malaysia from Marseilles, he began his two days of leave that the air force had granted him. It was his intention to spend time with his family during the day, when Farah was working, and then to be with her during the evenings and the nights. It was close to midnight when Farah welcomed Xavier into her townhouse, and he was pleasantly surprised to see her in a teasingly short nightshirt. He immediately got his hopes up, but these hopes were quickly dashed when she told him that he could not disturb her, as she had an early start to the day, and that she needed to get some sleep. Xavier was still content to be sleeping in the same bed as his lovely Farah, where he was able to steal a few glances at her, but her position on abstinence was strictly maintained.

Farah had some important meetings in the morning, but she agreed to take him to his parents' house on her way to work. As she was dropping him off at the front door, she decided to take the risk of being a little late for her meeting, so that she could say hello and spend a few minutes with Mirabel and Aldia. They were very much her family, and she always felt better when she could spend some time with them, even if it was just to say hello and to give a hug or a kiss. Mirabel was thrilled to have Xavier home, and she was also pleased to see Aldia's eyes light up when she saw him coming through the front door accompanied by Farah.

Once Farah had left for the bank, Xavier sat down to a lovely breakfast with his mother and sister. After listening to a lengthy description of how superior the F35 jet was to the French jet, Mirabel told Xavier that she thought the new jets sounded amazing, but that she wanted to talk to him about something outside. With that, she took Xavier and Aldia outside to one of the back patio areas that looked out over the property, and as Xavier stood there wondering what his mother wanted to show him, she turned to him and asked if he would like to have his wedding reception right here in the backyard. Xavier didn't hesitate to tell her that he would love to, and that he was confident that Farah would also embrace the idea. He then informed his mother that neither of them wanted a large, fancy wedding, and that they had already decided that they only wanted to invite family and a few close friends. He mentioned to his mother, sadly, that Farah did not anticipate having many of her family members at the wedding, aside from her Aunt Raja Noor, and perhaps a few of her mother's siblings. Mirabel told Xavier that she was saddened to hear that there had not been any improvement on the Hassan front, but she assured him that she would make a point of spending more time with Farah during the preparations for the wedding, wherever she decided to have it.

XAVIER HAD BEEN patiently waiting for Farah so that he could give her the good news about their wedding venue when she came through the front entrance with a downtrodden look on her face. Xavier had not expected to see Farah so distraught, so he decided to listen to her first, before he announced his good new on the wedding.

Farah explained to him that one of her sisters had visited her at the bank, during her lunch hour, to advise her that her ex-boyfriend had been spreading rumours about her to members of the Hassan family, including her father. The content of the rumour, as Farah explained it to Xavier—in rather crude terms for her that perhaps reflected how she was feeling—was that she had been sleeping with two guys at the same time. It was not difficult to see that the boyfriend was feeling jilted, but Xavier had to ask Farah why he would be so mean, especially when it was not true. Farah confirmed to Xavier that her boyfriend was not used to women saying no to him, and that he sincerely believed that she had been promised to him by her father. She also informed Xavier that he had called her some very unflattering names after he realized that he could no longer enjoy her intimate company, or any other kind of company with her.

When Xavier asked her about her family, she started to cry. She had told her sister what the truth was, and her whole family knew that her boyfriend had been sleeping with two other women when he was with her.

Xavier's comforting words, combined with the fact that he was there for her during this difficult time, made Farah realize how insignificant the rumour was, and by the time they'd climbed into her bed that night, she was feeling a lot better. The change in mood, and the comforting support she was receiving from Xavier, did not change Farah's position on abstinence, but they did both get a very deep, long sleep.

When Xavier broke the news to Farah in the morning about his mother's offer to stage their wedding in their expansive backyard, she was so thrilled that she almost forgot to thank him before she placed her call to Mirabel to thank her, and to accept the offer. She also made a point of letting Mirabel know that she was also looking forward to spending more time with her and with Aldia during the planning and preparation stages.

Xavier was so pleased to see the joy on Farah's face as she backed her Mini out of the driveway and onto the roadway before speeding away. Xavier didn't bother to go back inside the townhouse, as he was waiting for Lt. Colonel Lim to pick him up, so that they could travel together to the Subang headquarters, to get their transport flight to Kuantan base.

CHAPTER 6

arah could not remember ever being so anxious about a trip she was about to embark on though she had never had to endure a situation where someone she loved was in such terrible circumstances. As she waited outside her driveway gates for Xavier's parents to pick her up, it looked as if she had packed for a lengthy holiday, with her large rolling bag and her two carry-on bags beside her.

While the driver was loading her luggage into the back of the Suttons' van, Farah enjoyed a comforting embrace from Xavier's mother, Mirabel. Just as she was releasing her arms from Mirabel, Farah felt someone give her backside a soft pinch, and she gave a slight jump as she turned, pleasantly surprised to see the smiling face of Xavier's sister Aldia.

After apologizing to Farah for startling her, Aldia explained to her that her mother wouldn't let her go to Marseilles, but that she had let her come on the ride to the airport. She was looking out of the corners of her large, expressive eyes while she was speaking with Farah, as if she wanted to remind her mother that she was not happy about her decision to not let her go with them.

Mirabel, sensing Aldia's subtle message, gently pulled her into her chest, before giving her a hug and a soft kiss on the cheek. Then she gave her a friendly tap on her bottom and told her to climb in, they needed to get going.

Thomas was patiently standing back while these exchanges were taking place, but before Farah climbed into the van, he gave her a gentle little hug, and he assured her that they would get this situation dealt with, and that she should not lose faith. The drive was over an hour to the new airport, which was located well outside the city limits, and as Farah would often do when she was a passenger in any kind of vehicle, she fell fast asleep in the back seat of the van.

Mirabel and Thomas were both pleased to see that Farah was sleeping, and to see that Aldia had laid down with her head resting on Farah's lap. Farah's arm draped over Aldia, as a mother would do for her child. After Thomas turned back from the lovely scene behind him, he leaned over and gave Mirabel a gentle kiss, while he lovingly rubbed the top part of her leg.

The business class cabin of the Air France jet to Marseilles had only two passengers, in addition to Farah and the Suttons, so they had lots of seats to choose from, and they had more than enough privacy for sleeping or talking during their long flight.

Farah and Mirabel had settled into two seats side by side, while Thomas, who took a seat just over from them, was happily advising them that the plane had WiFi, which would enable him to make and receive phone calls and emails during the flight.

While Thomas was busy on his cellphone, Farah told Mirabel how adorable Aldia was, and how lucky she was to have such a wonderful daughter.

Mirabel expressed her thanks to Farah for her kind comments about Aldia.

"Thank you for those nice comments about Aldia, it means a lot to me, especially since I went through a bit of a tough time with her."

Farah looked over with interest at Mirabel.

"I hope everything is okay, she seems really happy."

Mirabel then explained what she was referring to.

"Yes, she seems to be okay now, but she gave me quite a scare when she started spending time with boys a lot older than herself. And I had the shock of my life when I was walking outside one night, and I heard noises coming from the guest house. I walked closer, and since the window curtains were open, I saw them engaged on the bed."

Farah was shocked and her eyes showed it.

"Oh my. That must have been terrible for both of you."

Mirabel looked a little embarrassed when she explained to Farah.

"I think I might have overreacted, but I was just worried for Aldia."

Farah wasn't sure how much to ask but she felt she had to.

"What did you do.?

Mirabel replied.

"I just yelled through the window for him to get off of her and for Aldia to come to the house."

Farah then asked.

"So how did you resolve everything with Aldia?"

Mirabel had a more content look on her face as she told Farah.

"We had a long talk about her sexual activities, and she admitted that she had been a bit reckless, and then she promised to be more responsible in the future."

Upon hearing Mirabel's experiences with Aldia, Farah reflected on how willing and open she became in her sexual activities with Amin, and how difficult it would have been for her mother to hear about them. She was relieved, however, to hear Mirabel say that Aldia seemed to have moved on from the promiscuous stage in her life, and that she was now behaving like a very mature and responsible young lady.

After they had finished talking about Aldia, Mirabel asked Farah if she had spoken to her family about Xavier's situation, and if they were aware that she was on her way to Marseilles. Farah did not enjoy telling Mirabel that she didn't have anyone in her family that she could turn to, who could help her with the situation she was facing with Xavier. But she had reached out to her favourite Aunt Noor, who had assured her that she was ready to do whatever was required to help. Farah went on to say that her aunt had always made the effort to stay in touch with her over the years, and to offer her some sound advice along the way. She explained to Mirabel, that her mother, whom she loved very much, had not felt either comfortable or experienced enough to talk to her about personal matters when she was coming of age, and as such, she had always turned to her aunt when she needed guidance, or just a second opinion.

Mirabel was relieved to hear that Farah had someone so special from her family that she could count on, especially in view of how poorly and unfairly they had treated her since she'd made her decision to her marry Xavier.

It was just before the cabin crew started serving breakfast to the passengers that Thomas moved over to Mirabel and Farah, who had just woken up from their long sleeps, and brought them up to date on all the news and developments that he had learned about Xavier's situation and what they could expect once they arrived in Marseilles. The good news he reported was that Suzanne Dupont, the advocate he'd hired to represent

Xavier, and the Graves Group, the investigative and protection services group he had also hired, were both now fully engaged on behalf of Xavier. The bad news, which he was reluctant to mention, but he knew that he had to, was that Xavier had been formally charged with sexual assault, and that he had been taken to the local jail, where he would be held, pending a bail hearing.

Farah, upon hearing this, asked how they could charge him when there was so little, if any, evidence to base any charges on. Farah and Mirabel both seemed to sag back into their seats when Thomas advised them that the alleged victim, Amina Chafak, had come forward and accused Xavier of having sexually assaulted her that night in his hotel room. Thomas tried to lift everyone's spirits, when he noted that Advocate Dupont had expressed her confidence to him that Xavier's bail would be granted, subject to a substantial bond being posted, and that he had also been assured by the Graves man that they would being doing everything they could to uncover everything related to Miss Chafak, and to discovering how she went from an incapacitated, unknowing victim, to a victim that now remembers every detail about her sexual assault.

As they all buckled up for landing, they were each separately thinking to themselves that the next few days in Marseilles were not going to be easy. But they also knew that they had to be strong and positive for Xavier.

FARAH HAD JUST finished drying herself after a long, hot shower, and she found herself staring at her image in the full-length mirror on the closet door, visualizing a scene where Xavier was in bed with Amina Chafak. Fortunately, Farah did not dwell on that thought for too long before she began to get herself dressed. She then made her way to the meeting which was being held in the lobby, with the advocate and the investigator.

When Farah arrived in the large lobby of the Sofitel Hotel, she saw Thomas and Mirabel sitting with an attractive lady and a casually dressed man, both of whom looked to be in their forties, and she quickly made her way to the private alcove where they were sitting. Suzanne Dupont, the lawyer, or advocate as they are referred to in France, wasted little time in letting everyone know that the prosecutor had agreed to an early bail hearing tomorrow, and that she had indicated that she was prepared to approve Xavier's bail, the conditions of which were a one-million-dollar bond being posted and the surrender of his passport.

After Thomas assured the advocate that both conditions would be met, she then let everyone know, that they should expect Xavier to be granted his release from custody, and that his freedom would continue until a trial verdict had been reached. With respect to the trial, Advocate Dupont advised them that the prosecutor had set a trial date for one month from today, and she noted that since this was an accelerated trial, both her office and the Graves office would need to assign significant resources to be ready for the trial start date.

When Thomas heard this, he knew that she was signalling to him that Xavier's defence was going to cost a lot of money, but Thomas did not view that as anything to be concerned with; he had ample resources at his disposal, and he was prepared to spend whatever amount was required to ensure Xavier's freedom. Farah politely asked the advocate how Xavier's defence was looking, and she responded that she felt that there was insufficient physical evidence to convict him of any crime, but that the accusation made by Amina Chafak would likely be the determining factor in the trial.

Mr. Roland Lemieux, the Graves manager of their Marseilles

office, then briefed everyone on the Amina Chafak situation, informing them that she and her family were Algerian immigrants, that her father was in prison on some flimsy terrorism association charges, and that her mother and brother lived in one of the rough, immigrant suburbs of Paris. Roland advised them that Amina had been living in Paris and that she was working for the PR agency that had been hired for the Delorme dinner, whose main business, he noted, was in providing pretty, young ladies for corporate events, and for private client outings. He closed his briefing by assuring everyone that his firm was now in full swing on the case, and that they fully expected to uncover the factors leading to her sudden accusation against Xavier.

While Suzanne politely excused herself, Roland remained so that he could go over the options for home accommodations that he had previously supplied to Thomas. Mirabel, who had studied the various housing options in some detail, advised Roland that they would like him to contract for the property located on the hillside, overlooking Marseille's ports and city centre. Mirabel then turned to Farah and told her that it was a lovely home that had plenty of rooms to accommodate visitors, with lovely grounds for outdoor enjoyment, and more importantly, that it came with a full-time cook and a live-in housekeeper. Roland confirmed the instruction and indicated that the house was presently move-in ready, and that they were free to take up their residence, at their earliest convenience.

FARAH AND THE Suttons sat nervously in the front row of the visitor section of the Marseilles courtroom, as they awaited the appearance of Xavier for his important bail hearing. The judge was the first to arrive, and after he was seated at his elevated desk, the side door opened, and Xavier was escorted in. Farah was relieved to see that he was in his civilian clothes and not in one of those demeaning prison outfits, but she could see from the way that he was walking, and his facial expression, that he was very dejected and sad. Farah and Xavier made eye contact, and he smiled at her, as much as he could, before being directed to his seat in front of the visitor section.

Mirabel put her hand on Farah's leg, as she could see that she had started to cry, and she softly urged her to remember that Xavier would be free in a few moments.

After a few procedural matters, which Farah and the Suttons did not really understand, since everything was conducted in French, the prosecutor confirmed that the bond had been posted, that the passport had been received, and that he had no objection to bail being granted. Shortly after the judge's statement, Xavier Sutton was granted full bail, but before he could join his anxious family members, he was reminded by the judge of the start date for his trial.

Both Xavier and Farah were crying when they finally embraced and told each other how much they'd missed each other. Then Xavier went over to his emotional mother and received her meaningful hug and kisses. Thomas gave Advocate Dupont a very heartfelt thank you for her work to get Xavier his freedom, before giving Xavier an extended bear hug. As the four of them made their way to the waiting van, they were a picture of happiness. They were not going to let what may happen in the future ruin this wonderful day.

As they drove back to the Sofitel, Farah turned a troubling thought over in her mind—the realization that her period still had one more day to run its course, and as such, she would not be able to give Xavier what he may have been looking forward to on his first night of freedom. Fortunately for Farah, she was able to refocus her thoughts, as she listened to Mirabel advise her and Xavier that both Dixon Wong, Xavier's long-time friend, and Farah's aunt, Raja Noor, would be arriving in the late afternoon.

Thomas made sure that Xavier and Farah knew that it was Mirabel who had orchestrated their visit, and that any credit, or any complaints, should go to her. Thomas then jokingly mentioned to Farah and Mirabel, that he was hopeful that Dixon had not been too bad of an influence on Raja Noor, with his penchant for enjoying the odd glass of wine and his engaging personality.

When they got back to the house, Xavier and Farah went to her room, so that Xavier could shower and relax. Before Xavier got into the shower, Farah told him that she still had one day to go with her period. He just smiled and put his arms around her, telling her that he totally understood, and that he was hoping that he would be around for a while, so that he might have another opportunity.

Farah moved closer to Xavier and held him extra tight for an extended period, to show him how much she had missed him. When Farah released herself from Xavier, she saw that he was in his finest form, so she gave him a tight slap on his backside and told him to get into the shower. Xavier, smiling, told Farah that she was welcome to stay, but she just smiled back at him and then settled into one of the room's comfortable chairs.

MIRABEL, IN THE kitchen, assisted the cook with the preparations for the Marseille-themed dinner of bouillabaisse and the other fresh fish dishes that she had organized for Xavier's homecoming, and for the guests arriving from Malaysia.

The doorbell rang, alerting her to the arrival of Dixon Wong and Raja Noor. The smiles on Dixon's and Raja Noor's faces, as they stood in the foyer embracing Farah and Xavier, clearly indicated to Thomas and Mirabel that the flight had been an enjoyable one, and that Dixon had convinced Raja Noor to share in his passion for fine wine.

Thomas was heartened as he watched Dixon and Xavier embrace, as it reminded him of his own close relationship with Dixon's father. Thomas and TK Wong had met and become best friends at boarding school in Canada, which was the same school that Dixon and Xavier had attended for four years.

Raja Noor, who was always dressed immaculately, had one extra button undone on her blouse, which revealed just enough cleavage to draw Thomas's keen interest. Thomas and Mirabel had previously met Raja Noor at Xavier and Farah's wedding. Farah had informed Mirabel and Thomas that her aunt was the black sheep of her family, and that in keeping with her nickname, she had lived an interesting—if not controversial—life.

As Farah and Xavier showed the guests to their rooms, Mirabel, who had been indulging in her own passion for wine while she was assisting the cook, took Thomas into the side study and closed the door. Without saying a word, she undid the buttons on her blouse and released the front closure of her bra, letting her breasts fall free. Thomas, who was now starting to realize just how much wine Mirabel had been drinking, asked her what she was doing. Mirabel sat down on the comfortable La-Z-Boy chair and told him that she thought he might be interested in having a closer look, since he couldn't see all of Raja Noor's. Thomas smiled as he went over to his wife and put his arms around her. He told her that she should never think that he had eyes for anyone but her. Mirabel kissed him, acknowledging that she might have gotten a bit carried away in the kitchen, and then she started to put herself back together. Thomas, however, had other ideas, as he lovingly took her hands into his, and he suggested to her that perhaps they could spend a little more time together.

It was a good thirty minutes before Mirabel got herself up from the extended La-Z-Boy chair and started to collect her private articles. Thomas, who was already fully dressed, was sitting in the adjacent chair watching his wife, just marvelling at the fact that she still looked as amazing, if not better, than when he'd first met her. Thomas could see that Mirabel was looking a little shy, as she carefully untangled her delicates, and he immediately got up and fully embraced her, assuring her that he could never imagine anyone being as truly special as she was, thanking her for being his wife. Mirabel looked into Thomas's eyes. She thanked him for his lovely comments, and then she told him that she was feeling a little embarrassed about how expressive she had been, and that she was afraid that someone might have heard her. While Thomas was quietly laughing, Mirabel asked him if he would mind letting go of her, so that she could get herself dressed before anyone started to miss them. Thomas and Mirabel were near the mid-century mark, but they were still very much alive, and very much in love.

When they went back out into the living room area, they saw that the others had still not returned from unpacking and refreshing. Thomas turned to Mirabel and said that they should have continued a little longer. Mirabel promptly advised him that he had already received more than he needed, and that she had as well. She then gave him a gentle tap as she hurried off to her room to tidy herself up before the dinner started.

Thomas and Mirabel were seated at opposite ends of the impressive dining room table, while Xavier and Farah looked across the table at Raja Noor and Dixon, who had the wonderful views of the city lights and the Mediterranean Sea through the large picture window facing them.

Raja Noor had changed into a new outfit for dinner, which still provided a nice view of her cleavage, but this time it was Xavier who got caught looking and who received a hard pinch on his thigh for his efforts.

Thomas, who was enjoying the lovely little facial expressions from his wife, mentioned to Dixon that he had recently played golf with his father, and that he had brought him up to speed on their expanding Luxe hotel brand. Dixon said that he was primarily focused on their flagship, Istana Hotel, and in trying to complete the many phases within their master plan for the property, while his father was leading their entry into the European market. Farah suggested they open a hotel in Marseilles. From her view out of the plane when she was landing, it looked as if Marseilles had everything a city needed to attract foreign tourists. Dixon agreed with Farah's assessment, and he advised her that he was going to try and familiarize himself with the different areas over the next few days. He then said, in jest, that he hoped that Xavier would be able to join him for his travels before the authorities had to lock him up. It was still weeks away from the start of the trial, so everyone was able to appreciate the humour and enjoy a good laugh at Xavier's expense.

Xavier looked at this mother and told her that it looked like she had lost one of her earrings. Mirabel put her hands to her ears, replying that it had probably fallen out when she was working in the kitchen. Mirabel and Thomas both had a noticeable twinkle in their eyes, as they looked at each other, while at the same time trying to control their sly smiles.

Dixon replied to Raja Noor's question about his family's hotel properties, that the Luxe group now had over sixty hotels in the group. She said that had she known how large the Luxe Group was, she would have been a lot nicer to him on the plane. Dixon told her that there was still time. Dixon always kept everyone in stitches. Raja Noor then delivered a friendly slap to Dixon's thigh.

Farah brought her aunt to the centre of their conversations, asking her how things were going with her Lebanese boyfriend. Before Raja Noor could say anything, Mirabel looked over at her and asked if he was the very handsome man that was with her at Xavier and Farah's wedding. While Raja Noor was affirming that yes, that was her boyfriend, Mirabel took pleasure in the dirty looks she was getting from the other end of the table. Mirabel was an amazing woman, as Thomas had recently been reminded of in the study, and she knew how to get her husband's full attention.

Based on the conversation about Raja Noor's latest love interest, everyone learned that Robert Khoury worked for two Lebanese brothers that he had grown up with in Beirut, and that their business activities were primarily in property development and business consultancy services. With regards to any future wedding plans, Raja Noor indicated that she didn't see anything happening in the short term, as she explained to them that Robert was always away in Europe, or in some other location that his work took him to, and that they often had long periods of time between visits. After hearing about her boyfriend's long absences, Dixon told Raja Noor that he felt bad for her, but Raja Noor—always quick with a reply—said that she was okay with his absences, as Robert always fully made up for it when he saw her.

CHAPTER 7

Everyone in the Sutton rental house in Marseilles was sitting around the dining table, waiting for the arrival of Advocate Suzanne Dupont and Mr. Roland Lemieux from the Graves Group. Since Xavier's trial would be starting in three days, Suzanne had indicated to Thomas that she wanted to brief everyone on what to expect in the trial, and to also provide an update on their investigative efforts. Suzanne began her presentation with a warning, which she directed primarily at Farah and Mirabel, that sexual assault trials are very graphic, and that many of the pictures and descriptions that they would see and hear over the duration of the trial might be quite unsettling. Mirabel thanked Suzanne for bringing that to their attention, and then she assured her that Malaysian ladies were not as sheltered as they were assumed to be. She asked about the trial being conducted solely in French, and Suzanne informed her that translation headphones would be made available to anyone who required them, as she had already reserved them with the court.

With respect to the court proceedings, Suzanne indicated that the first part of the trial would be taken up with the presentation of the forensic evidence, which would include any physical evidence at the scene, descriptions of the bodies, including photos and medical and toxicology reports. Suzanne indicated that she felt very strongly that there was insufficient forensic evidence to produce a guilty verdict. With respect to the witnesses to be called, Suzanne advised the group that the lead detective on the case, Detective Dube, was not on the prosecution's witness list. Thomas asked her why that was significant, and Suzanne replied that when a lead detective is not called by the prosecutor, it usually means that there is a disagreement between the two parties regarding the charges that have been laid. She went on to say that she had the right to call the detective as one of her witnesses, and that she fully intended to do so.

As Suzanne looked around the room, she could see that everyone was showing signs of relief, and even a little happiness, but she knew that she was going to ruin those feelings with the next portion of her presentation. Suzanne was looking directly at Xavier and Farah when she told them that everything, up to the point when the key testimony would commence, was in favour of a verdict of innocence, but she also made them aware of her opinion: that if the testimony of Amina Chafak was able to stand, then she felt that Xavier would almost certainly be convicted.

Thomas almost flew off his chair when he heard this. He wanted to know what was being done about this. Suzanne was prepared for this type of reaction, and she very calmly told Thomas that they were relying on the hard work of the Graves Group to uncover the necessary information or witnesses to counter Amina Chafak's testimony, or to give her reason to recant. Suzanne said that Roland would give them a detailed briefing on their investigative progress, but before he did that, she advised Thomas that she was leaving him a folder that contained all the evidence that the prosecution had made available to them, if they wanted to familiarize themselves with more of the details.

Roland began his briefing by telling them that his firm had learned some additional details about Amina Chafak and her family. He explained that Graves personnel from their Paris office had visited the suburb where the Chafaks lived, which the police referred to as "a no-go zone," due to the violence in the area, and due to the poor relations between the police and the immigrant community. He said that Amina's mother worked as a cleaner for one of the maintenance firms that cleaned office buildings in Paris, and that her brother was a low-level street thug, primarily involved in minor drug sales and small robberies. The father, he continued, was being held in the Fresnes Prison, located just outside Paris, under the draconian anti-terrorism law that allowed the police to hold anyone who even knows someone suspected of terrorism. Roland indicated that they did not believe the father was guilty of anything, other than the crime of association. With respect to Amina, he confirmed that they had visited the apartment where she had been living. One of the occupants at the address indicated that Amina did in fact live there, but that she hadn't been seen since she'd gone on a work assignment to Marseilles. The PR firm that employed Amina confirmed to them that their main clientele were wealthy Middle Eastern businessmen who wanted someone to show them around Paris. The summary was that they now knew the places where she would likely go and the people that she would likely contact, and they would be monitoring those people and locations as best they could. Unfortunately, Roland said, they didn't know where she was at this time.

He then provided an update on the investigation into the sales agents who were representing Delorme Aviation, in their efforts to secure the Malaysian jet contract. Delorme Aviation had been very forthcoming in providing the name of their sales agency, but it had taken considerable forensic accounting to determine that the beneficial owners of the company holding the agency were the Lebanese-born Khalil brothers, who were now domiciled in Monte Carlo. Roland, without getting into too much detail, said that the Graves forensic department was now working to uncover the separate company that was likely set up by the Khalils to hold the Malaysia contract.

Thomas, an astute and accomplished businessman, asked Roland to expand on that last point. Roland advised him that most military sales agencies set up separate companies, one for each contract that they held or were pursuing, and that the individuals attached to those separate companies were usually the ones directly involved in any activities, like the situation that they were presently dealing with. Roland's answer to Thomas's question, of when they expected to know the identity of that company and its directors, was that he thought it would be very soon.

Suzanne brought the briefing to a close, and she assured everyone that they fully expected to uncover more information about the sales agency, and about Amina Chafak. Thomas and Mirabel accompanied Suzanne and Roland to their cars, as they wanted to ask them some additional questions, without Xavier and Farah being present.

Thomas asked Suzanne about the weight that Amina Chafak's testimony would carry.

"I don't know why Amina Chafak's version of events has been accepted by the prosecution so easily."

Suzanne tried to explain the prosecution's thinking.

"I understand your concern Thomas, but the picture of an innocent young lady lying fully naked, next to the foreigner who had just raped her, gives the prosecution everything it needs to bring the jury to their side."

Mirabel, who was clearly upset by the prospect of her son going to prison for something he didn't do, offered some unfair and insensitive comments to Suzanne about Amina.

"I suspect that Amina has undergone breast enhancement surgery, and I don't think that having a tattoo put between your breasts is something an innocent young lady would do."

Suzanne understood the whole issue of blaming the victim, but she offered the following assurances to Mirabel.

"I understand your thinking Mirabel, and I will have our technical experts enhance the photographs and see if there are any scars on her breasts. But please remember that Amina is still the victim, despite Xavier not being the perpetrator."

Suzanne, again stressed to both Mirabel and Thomas that unless they could present an alternative version of what happened that night in the hotel room, then Amina's version would stand, and that would mean that Xavier would be going to prison.

Thomas then asked both Roland and Suzanne what they thought was the most likely theory behind this set-up of Xavier. Roland very clearly expressed his opinion that it was the sales agents for Delorme Aviation that had orchestrated the entire event, solely to remove a person who had recommended that the air force buy another vendor's product. He then assured both Thomas and Mirabel that they would find the person or persons behind the sales agency efforts, but that the concerning issue was time. He acknowledged that if they couldn't find the answers before the trial ended, then Xavier would be convicted and sent to prison. Suzanne told Thomas and Mirabel that they should make sure that Xavier and Farah got out of the house, and that they have some fun over the next few days before the trial started. There were going to be some rough days ahead for everyone.

After Suzanne and Roland had left, Mirabel and Thomas took a casual walk around the side of the house, to the backyard terrace. Thomas could see that Mirabel was a little teary eyed, so he put his arm around her and assured her that it would be okay. She told him that she felt so bad for Xavier—all he wanted to do was fly jets, and now he may have to go to prison because of some stupid jet contract. Thomas was reminded of how overjoyed Xavier had been when he'd told them that the performance capabilities of the F35 fighter jet that he had flown in South Carolina were like nothing he had ever experienced. They both agreed that Xavier was always happiest when he was in the cockpit of one of the air force jets, living out his passion for flying.

FARAH COULD SEE from the huge smile on her husband's face, as he held the controls of the Cessna 172 aircraft, that he was totally removed from any thoughts related to his pending trial or its possible results. Farah yelled over at him to make sure that they didn't crash. Farah had been on many commercial flights, but this was her first time in a small, single-engine plane, and she was certainly feeling her nerves act up.

Xavier's trial was starting the next day, and Thomas had wanted it to be a fun day for his son, so he very generously arranged and paid for a full day of flying for him and his reluctant wife. As they were safely flying along the coastline of southern

France, Xavier informed Farah that the fuel capacity of the plane would enable them to get a long distance away from Marseilles. He jokingly suggested that perhaps they should keep going and just forget about the trial. The air turbulence was minimal, and as he looked over at his nervous passenger, Xavier could see that she was looking more comfortable than she had at takeoff. She looked to be studying the multiple pleasure boats and yachts that were scattered over the Mediterranean Sea. This was the last week of the busy summer season, and from their cockpit views, Xavier and Farah could clearly see there was a good turnout along the coastal waters of Marseilles and its bordering towns.

Farah asked Xavier what the yacht looked like, that Dixon had procured for the day from one of his father's friends, so that she could try and spot them below. Xavier said that he didn't really know, but that he would take her in a little closer for a look. With that, Xavier took a sharp dive, causing Farah to shriek and yell at him to never do that again. Xavier apologized for the scare, but he reminded her that he was an accomplished jet pilot, and that those types of maneuvers were very safe and easy to manage. As they flew over the many yachts and pleasure boats, both sailing and anchored, they took note of the ladies topless tanning on their boat decks. Farah commented to Xavier.

"Some of those ladies would look better if they put their tops back on, but I guess everyone has a right to express themselves."

Xavier seemed to enjoy the topic that Farah had raised.

"I wouldn't mind if you showed me yours, and after all there is nobody that is going to see us up here."

Farah must have thought that Xavier deserved as much pleasure today as he could get, as she removed her t- shirt and bra and complied with his request.

"I know they aren't the largest, but at least they are attentive."

Xavier was most appreciative.

"Farah you are just magnificent, and I am so lucky to have you. Those men on the boats would be very envious if they knew what I got to enjoy."

As Xavier reached over and gently touched Farah's breast, she put her hand over his so that he would stay there.

"I can't imagine a time when I won't be able to enjoy your warm touches and your wonderfully, loving ways."

Before they commenced their turn towards the island of Corsica, Xavier advised Farah that she should just look for some crazy guy in a loud shirt dancing around on a boat deck with a wine cooler in his hand, and then she would know where Raja Noor and his parents were. Xavier was making his turn towards Corsica, but he also kept an eye on how Farah's lovely breasts moved as she turned in her seat to put on her bra and t-shirt. Even small moments like that gave Xavier immense pleasure – he loved everything about his Farah.

After completing the one-hour flight to Corsica, Xavier and Farah enjoyed a fabulous seafood lunch at the restaurant that Mirabel had researched and suggested that they go to. They both found Corsica to be beautiful; the people were much calmer and more relaxed than the people that they had encountered in Marseilles.

Xavier checked with the airport staff to ensure all the refueling and maintenance checks had been done before he opened the passenger door of the cockpit and helped Farah into her seat. Then he jumped in himself and fired up the Cessna for the flight home.

HAD XAVIER AND Farah been able to identify Dixon's borrowed yacht, they might have seen that their friends and family members finishing up a sumptuous lunch that had been served to them by the yacht's professional staff. Thomas and Dixon were showing signs that that the refreshments at lunch had been well received, but Mirabel and Raja Noor were not showing any signs that they had consumed a bottle of wine between themselves.

As they got themselves up from the dining table, Dixon suggested that it was time to enjoy the clean, blue water below. After asking one of the yacht's crew to throw over the tethered swimming raft, he removed his shirt and made the tall jump off the frontside deck of the yacht. Thomas followed shortly thereafter, but Raja Noor and Mirabel were still enjoying the balance of the wine in front of them. They had, however, removed their caftans, and they seemed to be enjoying the attention they were receiving from the appreciative yacht staff. They were still contemplating the big jump as they stared over the side and observed the men floating on the large mattress below. Shortly thereafter, the wine must have kicked in, as they both jumped at the same time, feeling the full force of the water as their feet broke the surface.

When Mirabel popped her head up and looked around for her jump partner, she noticed that Raja Noor's bikini top had not survived the force of hitting the water, and she started to laugh. While Raja Noor treaded water as best that she could, Mirabel yelled at the men to get down from the mattress and go for a swim while she collected the bikini top and swam with Raja Noor to the mattress. With the valuable assistance of Mirabel, Raja Noor was able to restore her coverage, thereby depriving the men of an extended view. Unlike Raja Noor, whose mature body was literally busting out of both the top and the bottom of her bikini, Mirabel was wearing a one-piece suit that very subtly revealed the shapes and contours of her captivating figure—while at the same time providing her with a dignified entry into the water.

After Raja Noor had been fully restored, and she and Mirabel had secured the prime locations on the mattress to do their sunbathing, they invited the tired men to join them. The refreshments at lunch had somewhat dulled everyone's senses, and they ended up staying a little too long under the sun, which they would feel the effects of for two or three days after.

DURING THEIR FINAL dinner at the Marseilles rental home, before Dixon returned to Malaysia, Thomas raised his glass to him and then he thanked him for being such a great friend to Xavier, especially during these most trying times, and he wished him a safe flight back to Kuala Lumpur, which was leaving just before midnight.

Dixon told Xavier and Farah that he needed to get back to deal with some pressing matters at his Istana Hotel, but that he would be back, without any hesitation, if he was needed. Xavier got up from his chair, walked around the table, and gave Dixon a hearty embrace. And then he told him that he would let him know when he could book their next tee time at their local club.

Thomas suggested that everyone take the remainder of the evening to just relax and to focus on positive thoughts, only. While Farah was walking back into the house, after waving goodbye to Dixon as he left for the airport with Thomas, Mirabel grabbed her arm and quietly asked her to meet her in the study in ten minutes. Xavier was on his way to the back patio, as he wanted to get in an hour on the stationary bike, so Farah felt comfortable leaving him to spend time with Mirabel in the study. When Farah walked into the study, Mirabel asked her to close the door, and then she warned Farah that she had something quite troubling to talk to her about.

Farah listened patiently as Mirabel explained to her how she had come to discover the tree tattoo on her aunt Raja Noor, and that it was identical to the one that Amina Chafak had between her breasts. Mirabel looked more than a little shocked when Farah explained to her that she had known about her aunt's tattoo, even before she and Xavier were married, but that she was not aware that Amina Chafak had one too. Farah informed Mirabel that her aunt had told her that she had gotten the tattoo at the request of Robert Khoury. Mirabel, bewildered, asked Farah why someone in her late forties, who was still attractive, would do such a thing to herself. Farah had an embarrassed look on her face as she provided Mirabel with her aunt's description of Robert and of his abilities to make her willingly do whatever he asked.

At this point, Mirabel opened the folder in front of her and passed her the blown-up photo showing the tree tattoo on Amina Chafak, which Farah could clearly see was in the very same place where her aunt had hers. Mirabel and Farah both agreed that regardless of how uncomfortable it would be, they had to show Amina's photo to Raja Noor, and then they would find out if she could shed any further light on the subject.

Raja Noor was very seldom at a loss for words, but she was silent when she looked at the tattoo on Amina Chafak, before she slumped back in her chair, looking lost. Farah did not want to stay any longer as she wanted to spend time with Xavier, so Mirabel suggested that she would discuss the matter with Roland, to determine if and how this information might help in his investigative efforts. Farah gave her aunt a loving embrace, and she told her that she had done nothing wrong, and that they would deal with everything later.

XAVIER HAD A real jump in his step and a noticeable smile on his face as he entered the dining room for his pre-trial breakfast. Mirabel, who was pleased with how her son appeared, held Farah back with a light hold on her arm, and then she told her how much she appreciated the extra efforts that she had taken to keep Xavier positive during this most difficult trial, and for keeping her own raw emotions in check.

Mirabel notified Thomas that she and Raja Noor were going to meet with Roland in the study to discuss a few matters, but that no one else needed to attend. Thomas had already been briefed by Mirabel, so he did not show any surprise or raise any questions in front of Xavier. When Mirabel joined Raja Noor and Roland in the study, he was showing her the picture of Amina and Xavier on the bed, and the blown-up picture of Amina's tattoo. Roland was not holding anything back from Raja Noor.

"We believe that Robert Khoury was very likely involved in the events that led to Xavier's arrest."

Raja Noor was obviously having a difficult time putting forward an argument against Roland's theory about Robert's involvement.

"I can see that Amina must have been very close to Robert since she has the same tattoo that I have, and I know the reason he asked me to get it."

Mirabel interjects, in an attempt, to provide some comfort to Raja Noor.

"Raja Noor, his actions were without your knowledge, and you need to keep that uppermost in your mind. I know it must be difficult."

Raja Noor's comments reflected her sad resignation to the events being discussed.

"I am beginning to think that I was just one of Robert's many conquests, but it is what it is. How can I help."

Roland wanted both Mirabel and Raja Noor to know that he would like to ask some personal questions that he felt were necessary, so that he could get a better understanding of who Robert Khoury really was. Mirabel put a reassuring hold on Raja Noor's arm as she described her relationship with Robert Khoury, including some very intimate and embarrassing admissions. She explained that she was always very willing with him, and that she found herself doing anything that he asked of her, including going through the extreme pain that she endured when she received her tattoo. She did, however, make it very clear to Roland that Robert was never violent with her, and that she had only compliments for the way that he had treated her. Raja Noor, as much as she didn't want to, had to acknowledge to Roland, and to Mirabel, that she now believed that Robert was more than capable of convincing Amina Chafak to play along with the set-up to destroy Xavier.

She concluded by saying that she was a mature woman who wasn't anywhere near as firm or as fit as someone like Amina Chafak, but that she still believed that most women would find it difficult to resist Robert Khoury's charms. When she asked Roland what linkages they had discovered between Robert and Delorme Aviation, he told her that Delorme's sales agents were two Lebanese brothers. He was waiting confirmation from the Graves forensic department, but he anticipated that Robert Khoury would be discovered to be one of the directors of the offshore company that had been set up specifically for the Malaysian jet contract. In response to Raja Noor's question about what she should do, Roland advised her to keep the communication lines open with Robert, but to not give him any indication that she knew anything about the Malaysian jet contract.

Raja Noor was scheduled to fly back to Kuala Lumpur the next day, so she would have the thirteen-hour flight to drown some of her sorrows, and to reflect on the embarrassments that Robert Khoury had caused her.

Mirabel was feeling quite embarrassed, as she informed Thomas of some of the things that Raja Noor had done, quite willingly, for Robert Khoury. She admitted to him that although she understood why women would want to experience what Raja Noor had described to her, she would never be able to look at Raja Noor in the same way that she had. Thomas shared her empathy for Raja Noor, but he reminded Mirabel that this new information was going to help Graves prove the conspiracy that had resulted in Xavier's criminal charges. It was becoming increasingly clearer to everyone on Xavier's team, that Robert Khoury was the likely architect, and orchestrator of the entire conspiracy that was intended to have Xavier convicted of the sexual assault of Amina Chafak.

ROBERT KHOURY WAS an avid wine drinker, and from his perspective, the more expensive the better, but as he sat across from Amina Chafak, in the trendy restaurant located close to his Paris flat, he joined her in drinking Evian water with their meal.

Amina was staring across the table at Robert, looking like someone who was deeply in love with her husband or boyfriend, and Robert was playing his part to encourage these emotions in her. He had even slipped a small box across the table to her. When she opened the red leather Cartier box, she saw that it contained one of the signature *Love* bracelets that Cartier was having trouble keeping in its stock. She got up from her chair and moved to give him an extended kiss, telling him she loved him so much. Amina had been pressuring Robert, ever since the conviction of Xavier, to find out when her father would be released from prison detention. He had been stalling, asking her to be patient, and he had repeatedly told her that the people who were working to ensure his release were also the people that were involved in the Malaysian jet contract.

When they got to Robert's flat, where Amina had been staying since returning from Marseilles, she advised Robert that she was now fully healed, but that she still wanted to know who had violated her and why. Robert very convincingly explained to Amina that Xavier Sutton was a privileged Malaysian air force pilot, whose family was extremely wealthy, and that they had bailed him out of numerous situations in which he had been accused of some form of assault against a woman. He emphasized to Amina that he was a handsome guy who was very attractive to women, and that he only viewed women as objects of his pleasure that could be thrown away when he was done with them. Robert didn't want to go too far with his fictional depiction of Xavier, so he suggested to Amina that what was most important was that he was now in jail, where he couldn't hurt her, or any other woman. He had been successful in getting Amina off the topic of her father, but he knew that it was not going away.

CHAPTER 8

I t was just one month before his wedding to his beautiful Farah, but Xavier, instead of focussing on the things that he had to do to prepare for his big day, was sitting outside the office of General Abdul Razak, the chief of the Royal Malaysian air force. He was not nervous about meeting with the top man in the air force, as he had had the opportunity to speak with him at previous air force events, but he was nervous about the subject matter that he wished to discuss with him.

After the General had congratulated Xavier on the high marks that he had received from the recent pilot evaluations, he asked him very directly what the purpose of this requested meeting was. Xavier very reluctantly began to explain that he had received an offer from a member of the Secretary General's office in the Ministry of Defence, just two weeks prior to this meeting. Xavier could see from the calm look on the General's face, that he was not surprised, even as Xavier detailed the perks and benefits that were included in the offer—which included training with an elite jet squadron of the French air force over a two-year period, while his wife would be employed by the IMF head office, based in Paris, for the same two-year term.

The offer stipulated that Xavier and Farah would be compensated on the same basis and in the same currency as the French citizens in those jobs, which meant that they would be making approximately three times the amount that they were making in Malaysia. In addition, they would be provided with fully furnished accommodations in central Paris, the use of two vehicles, and four weeks of paid vacation per year.

After listening patiently, the General suggested to Xavier that it sounded like an offer that would be hard for he and his wife to resist. He asked him why he thought he had received the offer. Xavier explained that he had received the offer only after he had submitted his recommendation to the technical committee for the fighter jet contract, and that he had recommended the purchase of the American F35 jets over the French Vitesse jets.

The General looked across his desk at Xavier. He told him that he had been with the air force for over thirty years, and that during that time he had seen many things that he did not agree with, but that he had learned to accept the reality: that other parties working on behalf of vested interests, often had more power than even the heads of the military branches had. He went on to explain that he was only a few years away from retirement, and that he was going to be following the jet contract very closely to ensure that the air force got the jets that were best for the force, and for the country. He looked very directly into Xavier's eyes as he told him that he would have to make his own decision regarding the offer that he had received to train in Paris, but that he recommended that he not sacrifice his principles for some short-term personal benefits.

As Xavier left the General's office, he had a much better understanding of just how difficult—and how disappointing— the process of selecting military equipment suppliers was. He started to think that Lt. Colonel Lim's promotion advancement was likely linked to a recommendation in favour of the French, just as his offer to train with the elite French jet squadron surely was.

WHILE XAVIER WAS dealing with his problems at work, Farah was enjoying a relaxing afternoon at her aunt Raja Noor's recently renovated penthouse, located in the city centre of Kuala Lumpur.

As Farah sat down to enjoy the tea and cakes that her aunt had prepared, she apologized for taking so long to accept her invitation and explained that her workload at the bank and the preparations she had been working on for her wedding left her very little time for anything else. Farah was both sad and appreciative when her aunt advised her that she had recently phoned her father to tell him how unfair and unreasonable she felt that he was being about her pending marriage to Xavier. When Farah asked her how he had reacted to her comments, she said that she didn't give him any opportunity to respond before she hung up on him. She had, however, received a very nasty call from Raja Soraya. Raja Noor expressed her opinion to Farah that her mother had made the call to her, almost certainly, at the request of her husband.

Farah informed her aunt that her brother, Reza, and a few of her sisters had been reaching out to her, but that they had made it clear to her that they could not defy their father's orders to stay away from her.

When her aunt asked her what had transpired between herself and her father, Farah explained the situation involving her ex-boyfriend Amin, and how her father had promised her to him. Raja Noor told her to just to ignore all the nonsense coming from her father and to focus on her upcoming marriage.

Raja Noor informed Farah that she was thrilled with her new Lebanese boyfriend, Robert Khoury, and that she was feeling like a newlywed herself.

"Farah you wouldn't believe how amazing Robert is, and he has my head spinning whenever I think about him."

As her aunt then described some of the wonderful moments she had shared with Robert and how amazing he made her feel, Farah was reminded of her own amazing experiences with Amin.

"He sounds a lot like my former boyfriend Amin. And although I have no use for him since he bad-mouthed me to my family, I still can't forget the amazing things he did for me in bed, and how amazing he made me feel."

Raja Noor was pleasantly surprised when Farah informed her about Amin.

"Wow! Farah I never thought of you in that way, but if he was anything like Robert, as you say he was, I totally understand why he had you hooked on him."

Farah decided to feed her aunt's thoughts on the subject.

"When I found out he was sleeping with two other girls while he was with me, I knew that I was through with him. But until Xavier came into the picture, I just ignored the fact that I was one of three, and I made a point of enjoying his company every day that I could. And he knew that he had me, and he made sure that I gave as much, if not more than I got. And I was happy doing all of it."

Raja Noor was clearly proud of Farah.

"Good for you for using him to your advantage, and I am almost certain he will regret losing you."

Farah however had a concern that she shared with her aunt.

"Auntie I am now concerned that Xavier is going to find me

too experienced or too accommodating, and I don't know how to deal with that."

Raja Noor was laughing when she responded.

"Farah, you must know that men don't care about things like that, and even though they won't admit it, they like women with experience because they know that they will get to enjoy it. Make sure you don't hold anything back from Xavier. Let him see how special you are."

Having put Farah's concerns to rest, Raja Noor took her hand and told her that she wanted to show her the most impressive part of her new renovation.

As Farah looked at the beautiful, cedar-lined sauna, and the massive shower and dressing area, she asked her aunt if she was starting her own spa business. Raja Noor confirmed that the facilities were solely for her personal use, and then she informed Farah that since there was no one around to disturb them, they were going to spend the rest of the afternoon enjoying the Finnish tradition of deep cleansing.

Farah was not used to the intense heat, and after about thirty minutes, when every part of her body was dripping with perspiration, she made her way to the showers for a cooling break. While Raja Noor was cooling herself under the adjacent shower head, Farah admired her mature, but fit body and thought how she would like to look that good when she reached her aunt's age.

As they were walking back into the sauna, Farah noticed that her aunt had a tattoo of a tree between her breasts. When Farah asked her aunt about it, she explained that Robert had asked her to get it, as it was the same tree found on the Lebanese flag. He had wanted her to remember that she was as special to him as his country was. Farah acknowledged to her aunt that it sounded very romantic, but she told her that she didn't know how she could have endured all the pain in getting the tattoo. As they settled back into their hot box, Raja Noor explained to Farah that the pain was incredible, and that, in addition to the regrets she now had, she was starting to feel like she might be kidding herself about Robert. When Farah asked her to explain what she meant by that, she simply said that she knew she didn't have the body she used to have when she was younger, and that Robert probably just wanted to enjoy himself with a mature woman, to switch things up from his collection of young women.

Farah found her aunt's comments a little confusing, since just a little while earlier she'd been singing the praises of Robert Khoury. Farah assured her that she still looked amazing, and that Robert should feel lucky to have the pleasure of her company. Farah then went on to tell her that maybe she was the one that needed to worry, since her ex-boyfriend felt the need to enjoy other women while he was with her. Raja Noor had to contain her laughter as she suggested to Farah that with her experience and with her looks, Xavier probably wouldn't let her out of the bedroom. Farah thanked her aunt for her generous compliments, and for her assurances that her past experiences could be very helpful in her new relationship with Xavier.

As Farah was taking a long look at herself in the changing room mirror, her aunt walked over and told her.

"It suits you and you should leave it natural"

Farah started to laugh as she brushed her hand over the area in question.

"I definitely intend to, but just so you know, I was looking to see if I had shed any pounds from the sauna experience."

Raja Noor laughed at Farah's clarification.

"Ok Farah, if you say so."

FARAH, WHO WAS now feeling much more comfortable, and a little lighter, attempted to beat the terrible Kuala Lumpur traffic by navigating a tricky shortcut to her Bangsar townhouse. While she was gripping her steering wheel with both hands, all that she could think about was how her aunt seemed to be under the spell of this new, impressive boyfriend. Based on what she had learned about him, she did not have a good feeling about Robert Khoury.

CHAPTER 9

he three judges behind their imposing desks at the front of the courtroom were looking very ominous to Farah. She leaned over to Thomas and asked him why there were three judges instead of just one. Thomas, who had educated himself on the French judicial system, informed Farah that three judges, along with the jury, was standard for all cases tried in the Assize Court, which only dealt with serious crimes that carried sentences of ten years to life.

Farah had to collect herself once she heard the minimum sentence, as she was feeling very uneasy with the thought that even if the three judges and the eight jurors to her right were lenient, Xavier could be going to prison for a minimum of ten years should he be found guilty.

As Farah and the Suttons adjusted their translation headsets, the lead judge issued the customary directives and guidelines to the prosecutor and to Xavier's advocate. Mirabel leaned over to Farah to ask her what she thought about the prosecutor being a woman. Farah's only response was that she hoped that Suzanne Dupont was an equal or better match. Mirabel could see that

Justine Arnaud, the prosecutor, looked like a normal, middle-aged woman, who likely had kids of her own. Mirabel thought about what her level of anger might be towards Xavier if she had a daughter of a similar age to Amina Chafak.

Prosecutor Arnaud called junior Detective Junot to the witness stand, and then she asked him to describe the scene that he found when he first entered Captain Sutton's hotel suite. His detailed description of the scene was not alarming to Farah, but when Ms. Arnaud held up the photo showing Xavier and Amina Chafak on the bed, she could see the dirty looks from the jurors being directed at Xavier. Their angry looks only intensified when they were shown the cellphone photos that the prosecutor had mounted on a large whiteboard and placed on an easel for everyone to see. Mirabel put her hand on Farah's thigh as she told her not to look, and then she reminded her that Xavier had not taken those photos, as the prosecution was claiming.

When Suzanne got her opportunity to cross examine the witness, she was very effective in getting the detective to admit that it was possible that someone else had been in the room, that they could had taken the photos, and that there was no way of knowing if Miss Chafak had been placed in the positions she was in, or if she was coherent or incapacitated while the photos of her were being taken. Suzanne's most important moment with the detective was when she got him to admit that, aside from the fact that Miss Chafak was mounted on top of Captain Sutton, there was no evidence of any sexual activity going on. The detective reluctantly agreed with Suzanne's assertion, that both Captain Sutton and Miss Chafak could have been incapacitated at the time, and that someone could have staged the scene.

The Suttons and Farah were more than pleased with how the first portion of the trial had gone, but they knew that the critical parts were still ahead of them.

When the judge adjourned the proceedings for a two-hour lunch break, Thomas informed Farah and Mirabel that they would take Xavier back to the house for lunch, and that they would also be able to say goodbye to Raja Noor before she left for the airport.

FARAH TRIED TO comfort her aunt while the limousine driver loaded her luggage into the trunk of the vehicle, telling her that it was not her fault that Xavier was in his present situation, that it was Robert Khoury who was the problem. Raja Noor was crying when she told Farah that she didn't know how she would get over this personal humiliation, but that she would do anything that Farah or the Suttons needed to help ensure Xavier's acquittal.

Mirabel and Thomas stood with Xavier in the doorway of the house, watching Farah go through the difficult parting with her aunt, and by the looks on their faces, they had considerable empathy for them.

THE AFTERNOON SESSION in the courtroom was quite tedious and boring, as both the prosecution and the defence presented their expert witnesses to talk about CCTV systems and detailed toxicology reports. Xavier would often turn and look back at Farah, with a reassuring smile on his face, as the experts slowly put the jurors to sleep with their technical descriptions and terminologies.

Farah did notice, from the prosecutor's questioning of Suzanne's expert witness on CCTV matters, that she could not get him to admit that Xavier could have altered the CCTV tapes. Suzanne's witness had made it very clear to the jury that someone would need to have specific technical knowledge to be able to erase and then restore the CCTV footage at the hotel, which had the three-hour window—between one and four o'clock in the morning—erased.

Suzanne was equally effective in getting the jury to understand that the amounts of Rohypnol found in both Xavier's and Amina's blood would have made them totally incapacitated, much like the condition they were found in by the detectives, and therefore unable to have engaged in any form of sexual activities. The prosecutor's contention that Xavier had Viagra in his system, for the sole purpose of having sex that evening, was dealt with very effectively by Suzanne's expert witness, when he stated that the Rohypnol would have rendered the Viagra totally useless.

Thomas thought that Suzanne was brilliant in the way in which she made the jury aware of the necessity to account for the items that Xavier would have required to carry out the sexual assault, as the prosecution had charged. She asked the jury how Xavier could have disposed of the items he used to deliver the Rohypnol to Amina, and to himself, and she also asked the jury why there was no condom, or any evidence on either of their bodies, that could prove there had even been any sexual exchange between them.

Thomas commented to Mirabel, as Suzanne was presenting her doubts to the jury, that he could see from the expressions on the faces of some of the jurors, that they were seriously considering her theory that Xavier could not have committed the crime, and that an actual sexual assault may not even have happened that night in Xavier's hotel room.

EVERYONE WAS ENJOYING their bowls of bouillabaisse, that the cook had specially prepared for their dinner, and based on the looks of satisfaction on their faces, they were clearly impressed with the cook's skills. Though it was also likely that her dish tasted a little better along with the feeling they all had, that the first day of the trial had gone very well.

As they were enjoying their coffees and deserts, Mirabel looked down at Thomas, who was seated at the other end of the table, and then she asked him how a simple contract for some air force jets could make someone want to violate a young lady, and then go to such elaborate lengths to try and destroy a young man's life. Thomas, who had dealt with some of the government ministries in Malaysia, in the process of operating and expanding his family's business, informed Mirabel that corruption in the awarding of government contracts was endemic in Malaysia. He then explained to her that the value of military equipment contracts, such as the Malaysian jet contract, was in the billions of dollars. It was widely known that the levels of corruption involved meant that the amounts of money taken out, or stolen, was in the range of 10 to 15 percent. Thomas could see by the looks of surprise on their faces that Xavier and Farah, like Mirabel, had not been aware of the quantum of money that was at stake.

Mirabel asked Thomas who the main beneficiaries of the stolen money were, and he advised her that the agents for the equipment suppliers, the corrupt politicians, and the ministry officials, including military officers, were the ones that profited the most. He emphasized, however, that the agents for the equipment suppliers—like the agents for Delorme Aviation—were the ones that orchestrated and controlled the entire process, and that they were the ones that distributed the money to the various parties. As Thomas explained some of the key elements of government corruption that Malaysia, and so many other countries, had to deal with, he could have brought the conversation closer to home, by using Farah's own father as an example of someone who profited from the endemic corruption. Hassan Ahmad would not exist as the wealthy businessman that he was without the existence of endemic corruption within the government. This enabled him to cream his significant share off the top of the projects he was awarded, while farming out the actual work being done to legitimate businesses. These same legitimate businesses could very easily have undertaken and completed the works without his involvement, and with considerable savings for the government. In the most basic terms, businessmen like Hassan Ahmad existed for the sole purpose of extracting massive amounts of money out of the government projects, and with respect to any other considerations—like the assistance being given to the Malays in business—they were simply window dressing.

ADVOCATE SUZANNE DUPONT was waiting at the top of the steps leading to the courthouse when Thomas Sutton arrived with Xavier, Farah, and Mirabel, and she asked her assistant to take Xavier into the courtroom while she spoke with the others. Suzanne explained to everyone, as she had once before, that this was going to be one of those difficult days, as there would be detailed commentary and speculations pertaining to the medical reports, which would involve explicit descriptions— with no regard for who may be listening. Mirabel assured Suzanne that they were ready, and as Suzanne turned to go to the courtroom, Mirabel wished her the same success today that she had achieved in the earlier parts of the trial.

The prosecution's first witness, who was supposed to be the Hotel Security officer who was on duty the night of the crime, did not show when he was called, and as such, he was found to be in contempt of court. Roland had previously advised Thomas that they had discovered unusual deposits having been made into the security officer's bank account, but that they had been unable to talk to him, as he had gone missing. Both Suzanne and Roland believed that he was an accomplice to the main perpetrator of the crime that Xavier was on trial for.

The second witness represented a very poor attempt by the prosecution to depict Xavier as some type of predator. She was one of the hostess ladies from the PR firm that Amina worked for, and all that she offered to the court was that she had noted how handsome Xavier was, and how he kept staring at Amina throughout the dinner. Suzanne wasted very little time cross examining her, as she felt that by putting her on the stand the prosecution had made their case against Xavier look very weak.

Mirabel tapped Farah on the arm and suggested to her that the witness probably had a cedar tree on her chest.

Before the medical testimony commenced, Suzanne was able to call Detective Dube to the stand, and she had very little difficulty in getting him to admit that he felt the scene in the hotel room had looked as if it was staged. Suzanne ensured that she made it possible for the detective to inform the jury that his experience of more than thirty years as a detective had led him to his conclusions.

When Suzanne had finished with him, and when there was no cross examination from Prosecutor Arnaud, she understood very clearly why the prosecution had not previously called him to the stand. Thomas turned to Mirabel and told her that if the rest of the day was going to be difficult, at least Suzanne had already made some strong points in favour of Xavier.

Suzanne's warning about the explicit nature of the medical

testimony was justified very early on, after the medical examiner—who had been called by the prosecution—described in detail what both Xavier's and Amina's sexual organs had looked like at the time that he examined them, and how Amina had likely received her vaginal injuries.

Suzanne very effectively suggested that since there was no evidence of any bodily fluids, or any condoms, that Miss Chafak's injuries might have been the result of her being penetrated by a foreign object. The medical examiner countered, in an obvious effort to support the prosecution's case, by saying that if Miss Chafak had not been adequately lubricated at the time that she was penetrated, then any average man could have caused the damage she'd sustained, if he was rough enough. Suzanne finished her cross examination, by getting him to grudgingly agree with her assertion that the injuries to Miss Chafak were more representative of a penetration by an exceptional man—which Xavier was not—or by a large, foreign object.

While this very graphic exchange was going on, Mirabel was holding Farah's hand, and she was feeling terrible, as she watched the tears slowly rolling down Farah's face. As Thomas turned to look at his daughter-in-law, trying to collect herself, he felt her pain, but he also took some comfort in knowing that Suzanne had done a magnificent job in demonstrating to the jury how unlikely it was that Xavier had violated Amina Chafak.

CHAPTER 10

It was a beautiful fall weekend in Marseilles, but Suzanne Dupont and Roland Lemieux did not get an opportunity to enjoy either the wonderful weather or the weekend with their families. Xavier's trial was consuming all their time, and since the testimony of the prosecution's star witness, Amina Chafk, would be taking place on Monday, they wanted to make sure that everyone knew what the strategy was. Thomas and Mirabel had explained to their legal team, that Xavier and Farah would not be attending, as they wanted to spend some personal time together and just forget about the trial for a few hours.

Before Suzanne briefed the Suttons on her strategy for cross examining Amina Chafak, Roland provided an update on Robert Khoury that did not provide any silver bullet, but it did offer some hope. Roland confirmed that Robert Khoury was in fact a director of the offshore company that had been set up by the Khalils to hold the Malaysian jet contract. The more promising news that he delivered was that the Paris office of Graves had uncovered old police records that indicated that Robert Khoury had been accused of sexual assault. The accusation, as Roland explained it, did not result in the prosecutor bringing any charges against him, but the file did provide Graves with the name and address of the victim, and he confirmed that they had met with her.

Roland spread his file out on the dining room table. He explained to the Suttons that the woman's name was Aafrin Mansouri, that she was an immigrant from Morocco, and that she was the daughter of the former Military Chief of the Moroccan Army. Aafrin had alleged, as Roland advised, that Robert Khoury had been sleeping with her over a period of six months in 2018, while he was in Morocco trying to secure a large battle tank contract from the army. Her father had been the chief of the army at the time. Roland went on to say that her description of Robert matched the one that Raja Noor had provided, and that she also had a cedar tree tattoo on her chest. Unfortunately for Aafrin and for Robert, her father found out about their affair. He promptly disqualified Robert's bid for the tank contract and exiled his daughter to live in one of his homes in Paris. Aafrin apparently tried to contact Robert once she was settled in Paris, but he had not made any effort to see her, and she had confirmed that she had not seen him since the last time she saw him in Morocco. Roland concluded by saying that Aafrin was prepared, and more than willing, to do anything that would help bring Robert to justice, or at least to have him feel some justice for what he had done.

After Robert and Mirabel had been given some time to digest the new information on Robert Khoury, Suzanne proceeded to brief the Suttons on her strategy for cross examining Amina Chafak. Suzanne explained to them that she believed, as she had previously advised, that Amina's testimony, on its own, would guarantee a guilty verdict against Xavier. She then advised that they did not have the important information required to bring

Robert Khoury to the authorities, and furthermore, they still didn't know where he even was at this time. Secondly, Suzanne explained that they still had no idea where Amina Chafak was, and, as such, they had no way of enticing her to recant her accusations. Suzanne concluded that she had no choice but to attack Amina on the stand, and to risk the negative feedback it may produce from the jury. Her main point was, as she had previously said, that if they could not counter Amina's damning testimony, then Xavier was going to jail, so the risk that she was describing had to be taken.

It was probably for the best that Xavier and Farah had not listened to the rather negative outlook presented by Suzanne. They had more important things to deal with, at least from their perspective. Xavier was talking to Farah as she lay naked on the bed with her legs apart and elevated by two pillows under her ankles. Anybody walking into the room at that moment would have assumed that Farah was either waiting for her gynecologist to examine her or that she was experimenting with a new way to excite her husband—but neither scenario was the case. Farah was following a formula that she had discovered in a book, which promised the best chance of getting pregnant. Once Xavier had finished making his deposit inside her, she had him carefully separate her legs and then place two pillows under her ankles. Now she was lying quietly for the suggested thirty minutes.

Farah and Xavier had made the decision a few weeks earlier to try and make a baby, and they had been diligently following Farah's formula at least once a day, and, when possible, twice a day. Xavier had told Farah that the process seemed a bit mechanical and impersonal, but she kept reminding him of the potential for an amazing result, God willing, from his efforts. Farah's formula had the added benefit of keeping both of their minds off the trial, and the scary outcomes that they may have to deal with.

THERE WERE CONSIDERABLY more spectators in the courtroom on Monday morning than there had been in the earlier parts of the trial, but that was likely due to the local press coverage indicating that the victim would be testifying today. A pretty, young Algerian woman, as a victim of a sexual assault by a foreigner, attracted the attention of the considerable North African community that lived in Marseilles.

There was anticipation on the faces of Farah and her in-laws, as Prosecutor Arnaud called Amina Chafak to the witness stand. The double doors to the courtroom swung open, and those assembled inside saw a very pretty and innocent-looking Amina Chakak being led to the witness stand by two uniformed gendarmes. Her dramatic entrance had almost certainly been orchestrated by the prosecution to leave the jury with the impression that she needed to be protected, and that she was very much the sympathetic victim of a terrible crime. She was dressed in a long, dark skirt and a long-sleeve blouse, that were in stark contrast to the figure-hugging dress that she had worn the night that she'd been allegedly assaulted. Her image of pure innocence was further enhanced by the matronly bun that her hair had been styled into, and by the limited amount of makeup that she was wearing.

Mirabel nudged Farah, and softly told her that Amina looked like she was dressed up to play the role of somebody that was quite different from who she really was. They were soon to find out, she had some very good acting skills to go with the look.

Prosecutor Arnaud slowly led Amina into her description of the events that took place in Xavier's hotel room, and she followed a very methodical approach, undoubtedly designed to allow Amina to recount her story while allowing the jury to feel the pain and emotion that she expressed.

She started by saying that, as she had entered the lift to return to her room after the dinner, a handsome air force man who was travelling to the same floor that she was on, asked her if she would like to join him in his room for a coffee before retiring for the night. When the prosecutor asked her if she made it a practice of going to a strange man's hotel room, she answered that he seemed so nice, and that he was talking about his lovely wife, and how they had just recently married, and then she told the prosecutor that she just felt that he was very safe. She then informed the court that she had gone to her room to use the bathroom before going to Captain Sutton's room, where she discovered that he had made two cups of coffee from the in-room bar. When the prosecutor asked her what happened next, Amina, who was now starting to look down, as if she was getting embarrassed, explained that they were sitting and talking about Malaysia when she started to feel very drowsy and out of sorts. For her next comments, Amina looked downward and lowered her voice, to give the impression to the jury that she was having difficulty with what she wanted to say. After her pause, Amina stated that she found herself sitting in her chair with all her clothes removed, and Captain Sutton was trying to pleasure her. She responded to the prosecutor's further questions by stating that she did not recall how her clothes had been removed, and that she remembered seeing Captain Sutton standing in a fully excited state just before he moved down on her. When the prosecutor asked her what happened next, Amina replied that she didn't remember anything else, and that the next thing she became aware of was waking up in the hospital.

While Amina was explaining her ordeal, Suzanne noticed a lady and a rough-looking younger man, that she thought matched the description that Roland had given of Amina's mother and brother. As she continued to look over at them, she told herself that it was very normal that they would be in attendance, but also that it was very likely that someone had covered the considerable costs for them to travel to Marseilles—perhaps the orchestrator of the set up of Xavier.

The lead judge, after looking at the large wall clock, called for a one-hour lunch recess. While Mirabel and Farah were waiting for the other spectators to leave the courtroom, they were looking at Amina and commenting to each other that she did not look devastated or humiliated. Rather, she looked like someone who was relieved to have completed a difficult role that she had to play.

The Suttons decided to take Xavier and Farah for a fast lunch at the small Italian restaurant located just down the street from the courthouse.

Suzanne and her team would be eating their sandwiches from the nearby deli in the small meeting room at the courthouse.

Suzanne confirmed her agreement with Roland's plan to put surveillance on Amina and her family, once they left the courtroom, so that they could find out where she was staying, and then determine how they might be able to approach her. Suzanne did not have to remind Roland, or any of the assistants in the room, how important it was for them to get to Amina, and to somehow convince her to admit to the conspiracy that she was a part of. Everyone in the small meeting room knew that Xavier was going to be convicted if they couldn't destroy Amina's testimony, and they needed her cooperation to do that.

Suzanne did not waste any time in letting Amina and

everyone else in the courtroom know that she would not be treating her as the innocent, young victim that she claimed to be. She started her dismantling of Amina's façade by telling her that she had noticed from the pictures presented in the trial that she had the most perfect set of breasts that she had ever seen, and she asked Amina what it would cost for her to get something similar done. Amina was completely caught off guard. She looked rattled as her eyes moved towards the prosecutor like she was looking for some instructions on how to answer. Amina must have realized that she was not going to get any help with the question, so she reluctantly admitted to Suzanne that she was only able to get her breasts enlarged because a friend had helped her pay for them.

Suzanne looked down at her own chest, as she was facing the jury, and she mentioned to Amina that her husband would certainly appreciate her having more prominent and alert breasts, which produced some friendly laughter from the spectators. Then she asked Amina how her Middle Eastern clients were enjoying her improvements. Amina advised Suzanne that she didn't understand what she was referring to, and at that point Suzanne informed Amina and the jury that her office had spoken with her employer, and that they had confirmed that wealthy Middle Eastern men were their primary clients. Amina quickly told Suzanne that she only went to dinner or attended shows with clients, and that there was nothing extra that went on.

Suzanne then moved on to the tattoo. She asked Amina if one of her clients had asked her to get that, and she responded that her boyfriend had asked if she would get the tattoo, and that she had happily agreed to do so. Amina would not provide the name of her boyfriend, but Suzanne was able to get her to admit that her boyfriend had been helping her recover from the assault, and that they were a very serious couple. Suzanne asked her how long she had been having intimate relations with her boyfriend, and if she was being intimate with other men as well.

As this difficult questioning was going on, Mirabel paid very close attention to Amina, noting that she would often look at the lady and the young man in the spectator section, whom Suzanne had previously identified as being her mother and brother. Mirabel assumed that that was the main reason Amina started to cry when Suzanne asked her if she was afraid that she might get pregnant or catch a disease from all her work activities.

Suzanne had successfully presented a very different picture of Amina to the jury than the one the prosecution had offered, but only the verdict would tell whose version they had accepted.

Thomas and Mirabel waited in the lobby for Suzanne to come out, and when she had arrived, he shook her hand, and he thanked her for a brilliant cross examination of Amina. Suzanne thanked Thomas for his compliments, but she urged him to reign in his enthusiasm, as she informed him that despite any doubts that she may have created in the jurors' minds about Amina, she still thought that Amina's version of events would prevail. She also informed them that, after the closing arguments were made the next day, she did not anticipate that the jury would take much time to reach their decision. That could mean that Xavier would be taken to prison, should he be found guilty.

This revelation hit Mirabel very unexpectedly. She grabbed Thomas's arm, telling him that they couldn't let that happen to Xavier.

Suzanne moved closer to Mirabel, and she spoke to her in a soft voice, to remind her that even if Xavier was found guilty, she still expected that Roland's group would uncover the necessary information to expose Robert Khoury's conspiracy, which would enable her to have Xavier's conviction, if it happened, overturned.

THERE WAS NOT a lot of conversation going on at the dining room table as Xavier enjoyed his last dinner with his wife and parents before the decision on his guilt or innocence would be rendered tomorrow. They were all satisfied that Suzanne Dupont had done a masterful job in the courtroom, but they also knew that Amina Chafak's testimony was very likely going to determine Xavier's fate. The closing arguments that they had listened to earlier in the day, from both Prosecutor Arnaud and Advocate Dupont, had been very eloquently delivered, but as Mirabel had mentioned, it was just a rehashing of things that everyone had already heard or knew about.

Xavier looked back and forth at his parents while he sincerely thanked them for being more supportive than any son could ever expect from his parents. He shed a few tears as he went to embrace his mother first, and then his father. Mirabel and Thomas were both teary-eyed as well. Xavier then returned to his seat and put his arm around Farah. He asked his parents if they would excuse them, as they wanted to spend some quiet time upstairs.

As Mirabel watched them walk down the hallway, Xavier with his arm around his wife, she had to put both hands to her face to mask the outpouring of tears.

XAVIER FINISHED DRYING himself after a long, hot shower, looking over to see that Farah was still lying on top of the sheets, in the same position that he had left her in some twenty minutes ago. Farah had made sure that Xavier enjoyed all her pleasures, and she had used all her experiences to ensure that she provided incredible memories that he could take with him to prison. They both knew that the dreaded guilty verdict was very possible.

When Xavier asked Farah if she wanted to join him downstairs for a green tea, she told him that she was visualizing the two of them, playing with their young child, in the backyard of his parents' home. Xavier thought that there was no way that she would believe him when he told her that he had just been reminiscing about their wedding reception in his parents' backyard. Farah not only told Xavier that she believed him, but she also suggested to him that it may be an omen, and that she would be praying that it turned out to be a good one.

CHAPTER 11

verything seemed to go blank for Farah when she heard the translator in her headphones say that Xavier was found guilty of the charge of sexual assault, and that he had been sentenced to eighteen years in prison, without the possibility of parole before he had served ten years.

Mirabel let Farah fall into her, and then she just held her, and let her softly cry herself out, until she was ready to collect herself and begin the difficult process of leaving the courthouse without her beloved Xavier.

While Farah was overwhelmed by her emotions from the announcement, she did not see the two gendarmes approach Xavier and handcuff him before leading him out the back door of the courtroom, without giving him the opportunity to say anything to his distraught family members.

Thomas could see that Mirabel and Farah needed more time before they would be ready to leave, so he made his way to the defence table where Suzanne Dupont was sitting with her head hung down. Suzanne had prepared the Suttons and Farah for what she had been certain would be a guilty verdict, but despite that knowledge, she was a competitive trial lawyer, and she didn't like to lose, especially when her clients were as genuine and honest as Xavier and his family. Thomas tapped Suzanne on the shoulder. He assured her that he and the family did not find any faults in her defence of Xavier. He asked her if she and Roland could come to the house in the morning to discuss the next steps that they would be taking to undo the injustice that had befallen his son.

XAVIER LOOKED OUT the small side window of the prison van. His hands and feet were shackled, and all he could think about was the way Farah had collapsed into the arms of his mother when she heard his guilty verdict, and how he did not even get a chance to make eye contact with her before he was led away by the gendarmes.

Xavier's thoughts about Farah quickly changed to ones of concern as the prison van pulled up to the imposing gates leading into the infamous Baumettes Prison. The imposing rock and brick structure had been built in 1936, and it housed over seventeen hundred of the most dangerous criminals in southern France.

The humiliating and demeaning process of Xavier's admission into the prison started with a full strip search, followed by a hose down shower in the presence of multiple prison guards. He was then handed his prison clothes and escorted to his new home, where he would meet his cellmate. Unknown to Xavier was the fact that the Graves Group, through their French judicial connections, and with the financial cooperation of Thomas Sutton, had been able to place him with a chosen, and cooperative cellmate.

As Xavier entered the cell that would be his home for the foreseeable future, he saw a middle-aged man sitting on the lower bunk. He looked to be southern Italian, or even French, based on his craggy, tanned complexion.

It was some minutes after the cell door was closed before Ange Colonna introduced himself to Xavier, and then advised him of the ground rules inside their cell. Xavier would learn later, from other prisoners, that Ange was a Corsican born, mid-level enforcer for one of the most powerful Corsican crime groups operating in Marseilles, and that his membership in the noted crime group provided him with protected status within the walls of Baumettes. What Xavier did not know when he met Ange was that his wife would be receiving a monthly stipend, courtesy of Thomas Sutton, for the services that Ange would provide in keeping him safe while he was incarcerated. In the weeks leading up to Xavier's verdict, Thomas had met with Roland, and they had discussed ways to keep Xavier safe from the many North African gangs inside Baumettes that would want nothing more than to avenge the injustice that had been done to one of their sisters. It was made very clear to Thomas during their discussions on Baumettes, that the gangs' form of vengeance usually resulted in a visit to the morgue rather than the hospital.

WHEN ROBERT KHOURY walked into the Khalil brothers' conference room in Monte Carlo, he knew he would have to answer some tough questions about the Malaysian jet contract, and that he had better have the correct answers. Abbas and Asad were not interested in any of the small talk that Robert tried to engage in, and that was made very clear to him when they advised him that they would only be discussing issues related to the Malaysian jet contract. Asad looked as if his eyes were going to pop out as he yelled at Robert, telling him that he did not like the entire business of the trial of the Malaysian pilot, and the risks that the victim and the security guard still posed for them. Abbas added to the intensity when he told Robert that he had never seen so many loose ends and such a sloppy job done, and that he was now doubtful that the contract could be secured.

Robert, the usually smooth-talking, suave salesman, appeared flustered as he stumbled through his updates on the hotel security guard and on Amina Chafak, but since he had been a friend since childhood, the Khalils seemed to be giving him some extra leeway. Robert had more success in calming the brothers when he explained to them that he had compromising pictures of Amina, and that they would be his insurance that she wouldn't talk. He gave the brothers further assurances when he informed them that he was keeping her in his private flat in Paris where no one would find her.

On the issue of the hotel security guard, Robert made it very clear to the brothers that if he sensed any wavering, then he would make sure that he was not able to talk to anyone.

The next concern that Asad asked Robert to comment on was how the Malaysians were reacting to the events that had taken place. On that front, Robert presented a somewhat mixed picture of the events. He advised Asad that the current Malaysian air force chief had called for a moratorium on any air force equipment contracts, including the jet contract, until a full investigation could be conducted on the Marseilles situation. Asad immediately jumped in, demanding to know if the chief would be successful in getting that moratorium and the investigation approved. Robert very calmly explained that it was irrelevant, as the chief would soon be retiring, and that he would no longer be a concern of theirs. He informed Asad that his friends in the Malaysian ministries had worked their magic, as they called it, to have the air force chief offered the vacant ambassadorship in London, and that it was almost certain that he would accept it. Robert explained to the brothers that the chief was nearing retirement, and since he was not a wealthy man, the plumb posting in London was an ideal opportunity for him and his wife.

On the issue of the chief's replacement, Robert was also pleased to inform the brothers that the replacement was a friendly party, and that he would not pose any problem to what they were doing with the jet contract.

Robert had been successful in calming the brothers down, and in getting them to believe that he could still deliver the Malaysian contract to them, but he also knew that he had exhausted any remaining leverage and good will that he may have had with them.

THOMAS WAS INFORMING Farah and Mirabel about Xavier's Corsican cellmate when Suzanne and Roland arrived for the meeting that Thomas had requested. As usual, both she and Roland were on time, and they had brought their positive attitudes with them. Suzanne looked very empathetic as she looked over at Farah and asked her how her first night without Xavier had been. When Farah told her that she had barely slept the entire night, Suzanne was unsurprised. She reminded Farah to never forget that Xavier was innocent, and that his exoneration would happen.

Suzanne's first order of business was to provide a briefing on what life would be like for Xavier inside the walls of Baumettes Prison, and what his incarceration would mean for them, as family members. Suzanne got everyone's attention when she informed them that Baumettes, as was the case at all the maximum-security prisons, had abandoned the established doctrine of rehabilitation, and that they had replaced it with the concept of warehousing. She explained that as a part of this new approach, the prison operated with the belief that mental stress—as opposed to physical stress—was the best way to control the inmates within the system. She did acknowledge that the inmates certainly endured physical hardships and internal physical confrontations, but she reminded them that since most of the inmates came from a world where violence was an accepted practice, they were very capable of adapting to the new forms of violence inside the prison. What the inmates had more difficulty dealing with, according to Suzanne, were the various forms of mental torture that the prison guards and the prison system inflicted on them, all with the intention of altering and controlling their behaviours.

She looked over at Mirabel and Farah to make sure that they were paying close attention to what she was saying when she stated that one of the primary weapons that the prison managers used in their mental war against the inmates were the wives and girlfriends, and, to a lesser extent, the mothers, and the adult-aged daughters. She could see from the looks of anticipation on the faces of Mirabel and Farah that they wanted to know how her comments related to what might be in store for them. Suzanne spoke very slowly and concisely as she explained how the visitor system worked at the prison, and how it was controlled by the management structure within the prison, and then implemented by the guards and other enforcement officers. Farah and the Suttons were silent, and they looked somewhat stunned as they listened to Suzanne outline the different ways in which the inspection process was imposed on all visitors entering Baumettes, ranging from the basic pat down inspections, to invasive body searches. Thomas then asked Suzanne if everything being conducted at the prison was legal, and if she could explain how the system was implemented. She informed Thomas that all their inspection practices were legal, including the most invasive ones, and that all inspections were monitored, with all videos being retained in the prison records. She also reassured everyone that all inspections of female visitors were done by female prison staff only, and that aside from some individual discretion exercised by the guards, all inspections followed specific guidelines.

Thomas immediately asked why they would retain the video records, and Suzanne informed him that they did so for two specific reasons. The first reason was that the majority, of the drugs being smuggled into Baumettes were found in the personal cavities of the female visitors. The second reason was to ensure the prison had documented evidence that they could use in their defence of any legal actions that were brought against the prison. In the interest of being fully transparent with Thomas and the others, Suzanne did admit that sometimes these videos of the inspections were viewed and shared within the prison system. After Suzanne had made them aware of what they could expect when visiting Xavier, Farah asked her how they determined what level of search was conducted on a particular visitor. Suzanne advised Farah that any number of factors were considered by the prison personnel responsible for visitor control, but the most important one was the message the prison management wanted to send to a particular inmate. She gave an example: if a prisoner was new, they usually wanted to let him know right from the start that they controlled every aspect of his life, and the best way to deliver that message, in their opinion, was through a very demeaning inspection of his wife or his girlfriend. She then went on to say that inmates learned very quickly that if they voiced any complaints about how they or their partner had been treated, then they could expect the next visitor inspection to be even worse. Suzanne then explained that when the inmate was being escorted to the visitor station, he was often told how the inspection of his wife or girlfriend had gone. The rationale behind that, as Suzanne indicated to them, was to ensure that the inmate knew exactly how much humiliation his partner had just endured as he looked through the glass barrier at her. He could then look forward to having the guards make comments to him about his wife, and how they liked or didn't like a particular physical aspect of her. Suzanne acknowledged to Farah and Suzanne that this information was very distressing, but she also emphasized to them that if they knew what to expect, then perhaps they could control their emotions, so that Xavier did not recognize any of the humiliation or other negative emotions they may be feeling. Suzanne emphasized that it was very important that Xavier not fall victim to the prison management's efforts to break him, as then he would be totally incapable of surviving within the prison system.

Farah and Mirabel needed to come to terms with and learn to accept the reality that they were more than likely going to be visually examined while they were in the most compromising of positions, and that they may even be subjected to some uncomfortable probing. Suzanne reminded everyone that according to the prison rules, Xavier's first visit would take place after he had been in the prison for seven days, and then he would be allowed one visit from his partner, and one additional visit from his parents. All subsequent visits would be determined by the prison governor, with the standard frequency of visits being one per month during the first year of incarceration. Suzanne looked over at Farah and Mirabel, and in a very soft and understanding tone, asked them if they thought that they would be able to manage their emotions during their visits with Xavier, now that they knew what was likely in store for them. Suzanne was not in the least bit surprised, when she heard them state, without any signs of doubt or reservation, that they would accept whatever humiliations that were in store for them. Thomas could clearly see from the exhausted looks on the faces of both Farah and Mirabel that they needed a break from talking about Xavier's case, so he advised both Suzanne and Roland that he would remain for their investigative updates, and then he asked Mirabel to take Farah for a walk in the backyard, so that they could clear their heads.

Roland was pleased to inform Thomas that the Graves office in Paris, through their close relationship with French internal security, had been able to electronically track Robert Khoury's movements outside the country, and that they knew that he was presently in Monaco. Roland advised him that they believed he was in Monte Carlo at the request of the Khalils, to either brief them on the recent trial, or to seek their instructions regarding his future actions. Thomas asked if they could now track his movements, as they worked to find a way to either have him arrested, or to have him interrogated by Graves personnel. Thomas's optimism from learning about the electronic tracking of Robert was somewhat diminished when Roland informed him that they were unable to track him inside France, as the electronic tracking was based on passport data, which only applied to foreign travel. Roland did assure Thomas that Graves was intending to put surveillance on Robert, once he returned to France, and that they hoped that it would lead to some opportunities to confront him. With respect to the hotel security guard who was found in contempt of court for not appearing under the subpoena served on him, Roland advised that his parents had filed a missing persons report on him. Roland believed that he may already be dead, and they were no longer considering his cooperation as a possibility in their efforts to incriminate Robert Khoury. Roland had left the issues relating to Amina Chafak to the end, as he and the entire Graves team believed that she was the key to getting Xavier exonerated. The team in Paris that was charged with tracking and contacting Amina would now be overseen by Graves' most senior man, and its leader, Yves Fornier. He described Yves as being a veteran of the French internal security agency, and that he had considerable experience in dealing with the immigrant community through his many anti-terrorism assignments. In addition, he still had access to informants located inside the dangerous suburb where the Chafaks live. The Graves team in Paris expected to begin surveillance on the Chafak family once they arrived back in Paris from Marseilles, and their main objective would be to find a way to get Amina alone, and then to work on finding her pressure points, so that they could use them to convince her to confess to her involvement in Khoury's conspiracy.

XAVIER HAD BEEN very attentive and cooperative with his cell-mate, Ange Collona, and he became increasingly aware, from all the menacing looks that he had received from the North African inmates, that he needed Ange's guidance and the protection that his status provided.

Sitting in a quiet area in the exercise yard, Xavier was listening and looking very intently as Ange pointed out the different groups and explained to him how they were affiliated and what level of threat or support they represented to him. Ange made it very clear to Xavier, that Baumettes was basically a jungle, and that there were two main species of animals—the inmates and the guards. He emphasized to him that they were equally dangerous. He informed Xavier that he had been in Baumettes for five years of his twenty-year sentence for murder, and that he wanted to impress upon him that it would be the mental struggles that would be the most difficult to deal with. The prison system was very effective in using mental torture to control the inmate animals. When Xavier asked him to explain what he meant by mental torture, he described some of the methods of humiliation that were deployed against the inmates, such as the visitor inspection system. Ange made sure that Xavier understood how the prison authorities used very demeaning and humiliating practices against the wives and girlfriends of the inmates, to ensure that the inmates knew who was in charge. Xavier was incredulous. He told Ange that he didn't think he could deal with that. Ange advised him to talk his wife, or to at least make sure that she was made aware of the types of situations that she may be subjected to when she visited him. Ange reinforced his point to Xavier by informing him that his own wife had experienced a great humiliation on her first visit. She'd had no pre-knowledge of what she was going to face, and it had had a very traumatic affect on her. Ange also suggested to Xavier that he consider asking his wife to stay away from the prison, at least until he had adjusted to his environment, and that he should start by telling her that he wouldn't be able to survive inside if he was always worrying and stressing about her. He also recommended to Xavier that he inform his wife during her first visit that he knew exactly what she had endured when she was being processed, and that he hoped she now understood why he didn't want her to visit him. Xavier asked Ange how he would know what she had endured during her processing and inspection by the guards if she didn't tell him. Ange said the guards would makes sure he knew.

Xavier slumped over, looking down to the ground as he contemplated just how he was going to deal with this news. The bell sounded, signalling to the animals that it was time to return to their cages.

CHAPTER 12

ves Fornier, from the Graves Group in Paris, looked like he belonged as he casually walked to the open park area where Akram Chafak was waiting to meet him. The hoodie, with the baseball hat and his beard stubble, provided sufficient cover for Yves as he navigated the tough immigrant suburb, without raising the suspicions of the crowds of young men smoking their joints and sniffing out any trouble they saw coming. Akram had agreed to meet with Yves, because the Graves informant from inside the Chafak's suburb had credibility within the immigrant community, and he had vouched for him.

Akram listened to Yves talk about Robert Khoury, and how Amina was being played by him, and even abused by him, just so he could make a few more million on a corrupt arms sale. Akram wanted to know why he should believe him, and what he could provide as proof when he spoke with his sister. In response, Yves suggested to him that he ask Amina about the tattoo between her breasts, and that he should then tell her that he had two other girls with the same tattoo, in the same place, that were waiting to testify against Robert Khoury for the injustices he had inflicted on them.

CHARLES THOMAS

Yves knew very well that the North African immigrant community was very protective of their women, especially if it involved
family, and that is why he told Akram that Robert Khoury was
almost certainly the person that had raped his sister, and that
Xavier Sutton was totally innocent. He suggested to Akram that
Robert Khoury had drugged Amina with a powerful sedative, so
that she had no idea that he was the one who had violated her.
Yves could see that Akram looked like he wanted to kill someone
as he absorbed the disgusting talk about his sister, and when Yves
saw these strong emotions coming from him, he decided to stick
the knife in a little further. He informed Akram that the other
girlfriends had informed him that Robert Khoury controlled his
women, which included Amina, by getting them addicted to his
special ways of satisfying them, just like a drug dealer does with
his drugs. He stressed to Akram that he could help Amina get
away from this guy, but he needed to get her to talk to him. Yves
didn't wait for Akram's full reaction, as he observed him clenching
his fists and narrowing his eyes in anger; he just moved toward
him, and, while handing him his card, told him not to take too
long. From his many years of experience working inside the
immigrant communities on various anti-terrorism operations,
he knew how sensitive situations like the one that Amina was in
affected the predominantly Muslim families; Yves was confident
that Akram would deliver his sister to him.

AS AKRAM WAS trying to deal with the information Yves had just
laid on him, his sister was pleading with Robert Khoury in the
comfortable Parisian flat where Robert had been keeping her
since the events that took place in Marseilles. Amina explained
to Robert that she did not understand why there had been no
movement in the efforts to get her father freed from his prison

detention. She also reminded Robert, that she had done her part by testifying to his version of events in the Malaysian pilot's hotel room, and that she still didn't know what had happened to her that night. Robert walked over to Amina, put his hands inside her plush bathrobe, and started to caress her expensive treasures, which very quickly took her mind off her father.

Robert was surely feeling the pressure from the Khalils and from the other parties involved in his efforts to secure the Malaysian jet contract, but for the next thirty minutes, he was focussed on reminding Amina why she would want to continue to keep his secrets, and to follow his directions.

THOMAS HAD A look of pride on his face as he sat in the dining room of their rental home reading the letter from Xavier that Roland had just delivered to him. Before reading the letter to Farah and Mirabel, as Xavier had requested him to do in the preface to his letter, Robert had done a first read, and he had been impressed with the way in which Xavier had made his points, so that the censors at the prison, who approved or stopped all incoming and outgoing mail, did not find any reason to hold the letter back. Xavier's first point in the letter was that he was very appreciative of the French books that he had successfully received, and he indicated that he would like to challenge all of them to join him in learning the French language. He thanked his father for making sure that he got the right kind of cellmate, and he wanted everyone to know that Ange was a wonderful teacher and someone he was happy to have on his side.

The next part of the letter was much more emotional for everyone, and especially for Farah, as he explained how he did not think he could survive eighteen years in Baumettes. But he was confident that he could hold on, at least until Suzanne and

Roland found the necessary leverage, or could convince the necessary witnesses to recant and to tell the truth, and he had full faith in them to be able to get that job done.

He addressed Farah specifically, asking her to please return to Kuala Lumpur with his parents, and he encouraged her to embrace her work at the bank that she loved doing, and to never think that she was abandoning him. He tried to explain his position by telling her that he could not get himself to where he needed to be, so that he could survive in Baumettes, unless he knew that she was safe, and that she was not spending her time worrying about him, at the cost of her own health and happiness.

The next part of his letter dealt with the issue of the visits to the prison, which Ange had very thoughtfully made him aware of. Xavier wrote that he totally understood if Farah and his mother were afraid to visit him. If Farah or his mother decided to visit, he would know exactly what they had gone through, so they did not need to feel guilty, or try to protect him from their humiliations.

To his father, Xavier could not thank him enough for the personal and the financial efforts he had made, from the moment he found out about the problems in Marseilles.

In closing, Xavier told everyone that he was feeling strong, and getting stronger, both physically and mentally, and that they should all be confident and know that he would never give up the fight—nor should they.

FARAH WAS SURPRISED to see that all the young ladies, and even the older women, that were lined up with her outside the Baumettes visitor entrance were all dressed up in fancy outfits, and they all looked as if they were on their way to a wedding reception, or some other special event, perhaps an anniversary dinner with their husband. Farah looked at herself in her very basic pullover dress and her running shoes, and she wondered why Suzanne had suggested that she dress down for the visit.

As Farah waited her turn to be called into one of the inspection areas, she reminded herself of Mirabel's suggestion, which had been to think about one of her fondest memories, and then to let herself go there, and to immerse herself in the feelings she enjoyed during that time. Mirabel, who had undergone a full visual inspection the day before when she and Thomas had visited Xavier, had told Farah that she was able to stand in front of the guards and endure their indignities, as she had successfully removed herself from the prison inspection room and taken herself to the luxurious Egyptian river boat that she and Thomas were travelling on when they celebrated a milestone wedding anniversary.

Farah did not transport herself to a wonderful place in her memory, as Mirabel had suggested she do. As she leaned over to fully expose her most private areas to the two female guards, Farah realized that she needed to face her humiliations in the same way that Xavier would have to face his during his incarceration, and in so doing, she hoped to be able to feel closer to him. Farah later admitted to Mirabel that she kept waiting for that moment when she would feel the guard's fingers inside her, but thankfully that never happened.

When Farah put her hand up to the safety glass to mirror Xavier's, she took a moment to enjoy the sight of his handsome face. He looked healthy and very much like he did the last time that she had seen him. She had worried that she would see signs that the prison had hurt him, both physically and mentally, but he was still the same amazing Xavier, and she was most thankful for that.

When they reached for their phone sets, which were hanging on both sides of the glass barrier, they couldn't control their smiles, or their expressions of pure joy and satisfaction. Neither of them mentioned the humiliating inspection that Farah had to endure, but they did remind each other about the wonderful last night they had spent together. Farah thought that the bell, signalling the end of the visiting time, had come far too soon. But she and Xavier had told each other what they had both wanted to say, and as she turned to walk to the exit door, after watching Xavier disappear into the prison area, she knew that she could return to Malaysia knowing that Xavier had not let his circumstances diminish him in any way

FARAH WAS ADJUSTING her seat to the lie flat position, on the Air France flight bound for Kuala Lumpur, when Mirabel asked her if she'd gotten enough time with Xavier to tell him everything she wanted to say. Fortunately for Mirabel and Farah, and for Thomas as well, they were the only people in the business-class cabin, aside from one Chinese couple on the other side. Thomas had made the comment, when they were buckling up for takeoff, that it must not be a popular sector, as the cabin had been empty when they'd first come to Marseilles as well. Farah adjusted herself in her seat so that she was sitting in a position that enabled her to look directly at Mirabel, and she told her that her visit with Xavier had been special, that it had given her the most wonderful feelings to take back with her to Malaysia.

Mirabel looked over at Thomas, who was taking full advantage of the lie-flat bed. She suggested to Farah that they try and get some sleep, since they still had seven hours before they were scheduled to land in Kuala Lumpur, and then she wished her sweet dreams.

As Farah drifted off, it was perhaps fitting that she took herself back to her most special memory with Xavier.

CHAPTER 13

It was December 8th, 2020, almost one year from the day that Xavier Sutton had met Farah Hassan. He was sitting cross-legged in the middle of the local mosque, awaiting the arrival of the Muslim imam who would be conducting the Muslim marriage ceremony called the Akad Nikah.

Xavier had not only put in considerable effort to study his religious books and to complete his conversion to Islam, but he had also put the time into practicing the recitation of his wedding oaths. The ceremony required Xavier to recite his marriage oaths in one continual statement, without stopping to take a breath, and he would be watched very closely to ensure that he had complied fully. When he had finished reciting his oaths, facing the imam, Xavier looked over at the two Malay men who were sitting close to him. He tried to read their facial expressions, as they were the two witnesses that would confirm that he had either completed his recitation correctly, or they would instruct him to repeat the process.

The imam, after receiving subtle nods from both witnesses, confirmed to Xavier that his efforts were successful, and then he showed him where to sign on the official marriage documents.

Then the imam made his way to where Farah was sitting, so that she could sign in her designated place, and after she had done so, he declared that they were now recognized as husband and wife.

Xavier looked very impressive in his traditional Malay outfit, the *baju melayu*, a two-piece outfit with a Nehru collar, complimented by a sempang (a gold-threaded fabric wrapped like a skirt over the pants), topped off with a songkok, a cap not unlike the traditional fez worn in the Arabic world.

Farah, who was sitting with her aunt, Raja Noor, in a separate section of the mosque that was separate from the men, was a picture of elegance in her white *baju kurung* wedding outfit, which offered just the slightest hint of her attractive shape. Farah's outfit was completed by her simple, tasteful wedding veil and her understated, heirloom jewellery pieces.

Xavier's mother Mirabel and his sister Aldia looked very fitting, as they were wearing their own full-length *baju kurung* dresses, the traditional Malay dress that was often worn by Malay women, and almost always when they were attending functions, or in this case, the mosque. They also had their hair covered by scarves that matched their outfits, as it was mandatory that all women, both Muslim and non-Muslim, cover their hair when they were inside the mosque.

Xavier's father Thomas, who was dressed in a traditional western business suit, looked as if his attempt to sit cross legged on the floor, which was the standard form of sitting for Muslim men in the mosques, had caused him a little stiffness, as he gingerly stretched his legs while he moved around after the ceremony.

Xavier made his way over to his best friend Dixon, and he told him that he was so relieved when the imam told him that his recitation had been accepted, because he had been almost certain that one of the witnesses would make him repeat them. Xavier always referred to Dixon as being one of a kind, and he was certainly notable for being the only person wearing a decorative batik shirt, which is traditionally worn by Chinese men at most functions, including weddings. Dixon had a mischievous look on his face as he told Xavier that he was very proud of him, and that he was certain that Farah would be much better for him than Alexa, the blonde, British architect he had previously set him up with. Xavier asked him to keep that to himself, as he went to speak to Farah's aunts and uncles.

One of the many wonderful aspects of Malaysia was how the various races respected the different religions and the various traditions and practices that were unique to the country's multicultural society.

Xavier and Farah's Akad Nikah ceremony was only attended by close family members, and a few close friends, and it was held in the morning, so that the bride and groom and their close friends would have time to rest and recharge before the evening wedding reception, which was being held at Xavier's parents' home.

After the ceremony, Farah accepted the warm congratulations from Raja Noor and told her that she was heartened to see that some of her aunts and uncles had made the trip from their homes in the western part of the country to attend her special event. Raja Noor, who was the youngest sister of Farah's mother and the black sheep of her family, was not prepared to let the unfriendly stares she had received from her siblings spoil her mood on Farah's special day.

Despite the obvious friction between Raja Noor and her siblings, Farah was pleased that she had some close relatives to share her special moment with, since her immediate family members were not in attendance. As she circulated amongst the guests, accepting their congratulations, Farah told herself that her mother and sisters would have been in attendance today had it not been for the position that her dictatorial and unreasonable father had taken regarding her marriage to Xavier.

JAMES SUTTON, WHO was Thomas Sutton's older brother from Canada, was wearing one of Thomas's oversized Panama hats as he sat on one of the comfortable pool loungers, enjoying his second martini of the day. He was joined by his son-in-law, Gordon Brown, and the two Soliano brothers, Mirabel Sutton's younger brothers, who were keeping pace with James in the martini category. They all watched their wives enjoying themselves, both in the pool and on the pool deck. The two Soliano wives were showing everyone that they could still do handstands in their early forties, while James' wife, Sarah, and his daughter, Emily, were sunning themselves on the flagstone pool deck. The Soliano brothers were both wearing sunglasses, which helped them to disguise their frequent glances over at the two Canadian ladies, who were quite noticeable in their small bikinis.

Thomas, who had returned from the Akad Nikah ceremony and changed into his pool shorts and a comfortable t-shirt, made his way out to the pool. As he approached the pool deck, he asked his older brother James if he was enjoying his Panama hat and the ample supply of refreshments at his disposal. The caterers, who were busy setting up for the evening wedding reception, had already stocked the bar that they had established beside the pool pavilion building. James and the Solianos had been sampling the offerings. James raised his glass to Thomas and said he was thinking of moving to Malaysia. Thomas quickly reminded him that he had just been named one of Canada's top fifty businessmen, and that the Sutton Group needed his continued leadership at the head office in Oakville.

James, like his brother, was fully supportive of Xavier marrying Farah, and he had already extended his, and his wife's, open invitation to Farah, for her and Xavier to come and stay with them in Canada, whenever they wanted.

Just as Thomas was telling his brother that Sarah still looked amazing, Mirabel, who had also changed into a cooling pair of shorts, arrived, and with a slight smile on her face, she pointed at all the men, and she told them they had better take it easy—she didn't want to see any bad behaviour during Xavier's wedding reception. She then leaned over and gave James some nice kisses on both cheeks before walking over to talk to Sarah and Emily.

Mirabel did not spend much time with Sarah, as she wanted to survey all the work being done by the caterers and the event company for the evening reception.

Thomas and James were reminding each other how lucky they were to have such special wives when Aldia arrived on the scene, dressed as if she were going for a jog in the neighbourhood. James, who adored his niece, stood up and gave her a big hug, and then he asked her to sit down and talk to her favourite uncle for a few moments. He proceeded to ask her why her father, who was presently enjoying the scene of his older brother talking to Aldia, with his arm holding her close, did not have her working with him in the family company. Aldia replied that he had never asked her, but that if he did, she would love to. Thomas, listening in, was surprised—he had never thought Aldia would want to work in the Sutton Group. He had mentioned to his wife, on numerous occasions, that he would welcome Aldia inside the company if she expressed an interest, especially since their only other child was a pilot for life.

James didn't have to remind Thomas that their international operations, which Thomas ran from Kuala Lumpur, were quickly approaching the size of the North American operations, which James and his two sons managed out of their Canadian headquarters. Aldia asked her uncle to keep working on her dad as she gave him a peck on the cheek, and then she informed them that she had to get back to Farah's townhouse to help her get ready for her wedding reception.

The wedding planners that Mirabel and Farah had engaged for the reception had ensured that every detail was looked after, and that started at the gates to the Sutton estate, where uniformed valet staff met the arriving guests and directed them to parking spaces along the quiet streets around the property. Other staff ferried the guests from their cars, via double seated golf carts, to the main house. When the guests arrived in the expansive backyard, they were met with a sea of white, from the tablecloths on the circular table and chair settings that had been assembled amongst the trees and flowering plants. Special event lighting helped create the welcoming mood that both Farah and Mirabel had requested. As the guests mingled around the pool deck area, enjoying their cocktails and fruit juices, they noticed the many small, blue lights flashing around the property, which were coming from the multitude of mosquito zappers that had been deployed, to ensure that any unwanted pests were kept safely away from the guests. The number of people attending the reception was under fifty, as Xavier and Farah had intended, but the sounds of applause announcing the arrival of the bride and groom suggested that the attendance was something greater than that number. Farah was now dressed in a more fitted version of the *baju kurung* that she'd worn for the mosque ceremony, whereas Xavier had adopted a traditional black-tie tuxedo, and as they made their way to the head table, they garnered the full admiration of the guests for their appearance and for their friendly smiles.

Mirabel had arranged for a small string quartet to provide some soft background music, but they were often drowned out by the enthusiasm from some of the tables whenever the happy couple complied with the guests' wishes for a wedding kiss. Not surprisingly, most of the noise was coming from the tables with the men who had earlier in the day been enjoying their martinis.

The guests, including the few raucous ones, respectfully stopped their conversations and listened as Farah's uncle, who was her mother's oldest brother, prepared to deliver his speech. He began by thanking the Suttons for their exceptional hospitality, and for welcoming their precious Farah into their family. As he looked very lovingly over at Farah and Xavier, he told everyone, but most specifically the happy couple, that Farah's mother could not attend due to circumstances beyond her control, but that she wanted him to tell them that she wished them more happiness than they could ever imagine, and that she hoped that they could one day find a way to forgive her.

Xavier leaned over to give Farah a reassuring hug and a kiss, as he could see that she had tears in her eyes.

Thomas very warmly shook Farah's uncle's hand, and he thanked him for extending the kind words that he had just delivered, as he exchanged places with him at the lectern. Thomas began his speech by thanking his lovely wife Mirabel for once again making everything so perfect, and for enabling him to enjoy the type of rewarding marriage that he now wished for his only son and his special bride. He then turned his head slightly, so that he was looking directly at Xavier and Farah, and he told them that the Suttons would always consider Farah one of their own, and that they could always count on them if they were ever in need, in the good times, but more importantly in the difficult times, and when things looked like they couldn't get any worse. As everyone rose from their seats to raise their glasses to the bride and groom, Thomas told Farah and Xavier to fly high, but to never let the other person down.

Farah and Xavier decided that they would make the rounds to express their thanks at each of the tables, and their first stop was at Raja Noor's table, which also included the two Soliano brothers and their wives. As she very warmly embraced her favourite niece, Raja Noor told her that not only did she look like the prized jewel of the Hassan family, but that she and her handsome pilot looked like a prince and princess from a Disney production.

Robert Khoury, Raja Noor's handsome boyfriend, very elegantly leaned over and kissed Farah on each cheek as he congratulated her on her special day, and then he gave Xavier a slight embrace while he wished him every happiness in his married life.

As they made their way over to Dixon Wong's table, Farah whispered to Xavier that there was something too smooth about Robert Khoury, something that she just didn't like. Xavier suggested to her that he seemed like a perfect gentleman to him, and then he reminded Farah that her aunt was looking very happy as she stood next to him.

Dixon had a young Chinese woman sitting beside him. She looked very happy to be with him, but Xavier had noticed that Dixon seemed unusually quiet; he wasn't moving around as he normally did. After giving it some further thought, he realized that Dixon's father, TK, and his mother, Daisy, were at the table with him, and that the young lady was likely the one that they expected him to marry. After Dixon's guest had retaken her seat, Xavier quietly asked Dixon if she was the one, as he had been hearing Dixon's complaints about her for months. Dixon gave him a nod and a look of sad resignation.

Farah told Xavier that Dixon's date was lovely, and that he should be very happy with her. Xavier wanted to tell Farah about Dixon's true love, but he thought it was best to keep that between Dixon and himself. Despite what appeared to be a somewhat arranged marriage that was being forced on him, Dixon got along very well with his father, and they worked together very effectively in the running of their sizeable luxury hotel empire. Before Xavier and Farah could move on to the next table, Dixon informed them that he had been assured by his hotel manager that their honeymoon suite at the Istana Hotel was ready and waiting for them, and Farah, with a look of pure innocence on her face, thanked Dixon and assured him that they were looking forward to it.

FARAH WAS HANGING up her wedding outfit and getting herself ready to join Xavier in the suite's whirlpool bath when he yelled out to her that they could have invited guests, as there was enough room in the bath to fit another eight people. The presidential suite in the Istana Hotel, the crown jewel in Dixon's family's hotel group, had every luxury you could imagine, including an unobstructed view of the Kuala Lumpur skyline, which you could take in while enjoying your bath.

As Farah hung her bathrobe on the wall hook and slowly stepped up to enter the mass of bubbles below her, Xavier got an extended first look at what she had been hiding from him over their year-long engagement. When Xavier's eyes met Farah's eyes, he could see that she was quite confident that she would live up to his expectations. In fact, those first glimpses of Farah's magnificent, natural beauty were images that would remain in Xavier's mind forever; the look of pure pleasure on his face was clear evidence of that. Farah had yet to see her husband in the same way, as he was protected by what seemed to be an increasing amount of bath bubbles.

As they were exchanging stories about the evening's success, and about the different guests that they had spent time with, Xavier asked Farah why she kept giggling. She told him that the whirlpool jets were doing his work for him.

LATER, FARAH AND Xavier engaged in some playful discussions about how their first night as husband and wife had gone. Farah gave Xavier a good wack on the arm after he indicated to her that he couldn't really tell how things had gone, and that he thought they should perhaps jump back into the bed and recreate the moment, so that he could be certain. But they both knew how amazing the night had been, and that there was very little room for improvement from either party.

CHAPTER 14

Yves was being quite direct with the informant he had inside the Aulnay-sous-Bois suburb, as he had not heard back from either Akram Chafak or Amina Chafak, and it had been over two weeks since he had met with Akram. All that the informant was able to tell Yves was that Akram was going crazy trying to find out where Robert Khoury was located, as he said he wanted to kill him for what he had done to his sister. With respect to Amina, the informant advised Yves that he had seen Amina a few days earlier, and that she had started to wear a head scarf and dress very conservatively. Yves and his team at the Paris office agreed that they needed to go to the area where Amina had been seen and wait for an opportunity to talk to her. If she was not willing to talk to them, then they had to be prepared to snatch her.

Roland, from the Marseilles office of Graves, had informed Yves that the body of the missing security guard from the Marseilles hotel had washed up on the rocks just outside the Toulon coastal area, which was about sixty kilometers from Marseilles. The report Roland received was that there was no evidence of foul play, but both he and Yves knew that it was likely the work of Robert Khoury.

They knew that Amina Chafak represented their best chance to get Xavier's conviction overturned, as they believed that Robert Khoury would probably go underground in Lebanon, if he hadn't already done so, and that it would be very difficult to find him there.

AS THE INFORMANT hustled Amina into the beaten-up van, Yves calmly drove out of the suburb to a company-owned flat in Paris that they often used for clients who wanted to stay under the radar, or for situations like the one that they were presently dealing with.

After Amina had calmed down, and Yves had convinced her that she was in no danger, she started to explain her break from Robert Khoury, and about all the guilt that she was carrying for how she had embarrassed herself in the eyes of her brother, and for her role in putting an innocent man in prison. She confessed to Yves that Robert had convinced her that he could get her father out of prison, and he had told her that if she could just help him with the situation at the hotel in Marseilles, then he would guarantee that her father would be returned home. Robert had assured her that it would all be done within one week from the day that the Malaysian was convicted of raping her.

Yves tried to get a better understanding of how much control that Robert had over her, and if he still did, and it became very clear to him, based on the information that Amina was providing him, that she believed that Robert was going to marry her. He felt a great deal of sympathy for Amina, however, when she told him that the night before she'd snuck away from Robert's Paris flat, he'd been quite rough with her; he had never previously treated her like that. Yves knew that Amina lived a life that involved frequent encounters with men, but he could see that she had the look of someone who was fearful.

It was important that Yves get Amina to explain how she'd found herself in Xavier's hotel room that night in Marseilles, as he needed to understand if there were other players involved. Amina was very cooperative; she explained that when she'd returned to her hotel room, after the Delorme Aviation dinner, Robert had been sitting in her room with two glasses of wine on the sitting room table. They'd shared the wine and some talk about their future together in Lebanon; Robert had always told her that he wanted to start a life with her in his home country. And then they went to bed and enjoyed each other's company. Amina said that the last thing she remembered was that Robert had entered her from behind, and then she woke up in the hospital room.

Yves did not feel comfortable with the idea of Amina returning home to her family's apartment, so he asked her if she would be willing to stay at the flat where she was now. When she agreed to do so, he assured her that he would have one of their female staff stay with her, who would look after everything that she needed. He encouraged Amina to phone her mother and to explain everything to her, but he did request that she keep her location a secret.

After Yves received Amina's firm commitment to recant her testimony to the Marseilles prosecutor, he immediately phoned Roland at the Marseilles office to give him the good news.

Before Roland could hang up the phone to call the Suttons, Yves told him he wanted to work up a plan that would convince the Khalils to meet with him. Roland was confused; why would he want to meet with them, but after Yves explained his logic, it made perfect sense, and it reminded Roland why everyone wanted Yves' assistance on their cases. Yves wanted to put some fear into the Khalils about the damage that Robert Khoury was doing to their business and to their overall reputation. If the Khalils could be convinced that Khoury was causing irreparable damage to them and their businesses, then they would likely take the necessary steps to distance themselves from him. Yves suggested to Roland that in this scenario the Khalils would ultimately force Robert to put all his energy into saving his own skin, instead of controlling Amina and protecting his conspiracy against Xavier. The challenge, as Yves explained it to Roland, was to come up with a believable story that would entice the Khalils into agreeing to meet with him. As they closed out their call, they both agreed to give some thought to developing a story to present to the Khalils, within the next few weeks.

FARAH WAS BUSY going over reports at her desk in the Central Bank building when her boss walked into her office and reminded her that it was well past the dinner hour, and that she should really go home. Farah felt like she was getting back to normal, or at least as much as she could. Knowing that Xavier was safe and settled into the life he had to live for now, she felt content and able to move forward. She was fortunate to have the efficient service of the Graves office in Marseilles, who ensured a smooth and quick delivery of letters between Xavier and Farah. Farah would email her letters to the Grave's office, where they would print them out, and then deliver them to the prison. In the other direction, they would collect Xavier's letters, scan them, and then email them to Farah. Farah shared many of Xavier's letters with Mirabel and Thomas, and they were very relieved to read that he was starting to make some new friends, under Ange's guidance, and that he felt more comfortable within the general prison population. Farah felt a little guilty, however, when he advised her that he was speaking French on a more regular basis with Ange, and that he felt he would be relatively fluent in French within a few months. Farah had not been as diligent with her language work as Xavier had been, and she was reluctant to tell him, but she also knew that, unfortunately, she still had some time to make up for her lack of effort.

RAJA NOOR WAS touching and moving all the items on the restaurant table as she nervously waited for Farah to join her for their first meeting since the embarrassing moments she'd experienced in Marseilles. Farah had been very busy getting back up to speed at work, but she had also used that as an excuse to keep putting her aunt off, as she needed some time to remind herself of the fact that her aunt had done nothing wrong, other than get sucked in by a terrible man. As Farah entered the restaurant and hustled to the table, her aunt was already on her feet, ready to give her a long overdue hug and kiss. Their first moment together was not as awkward as they'd both thought it would be, and before long they were in full conversation about their lives, and about where things stood in Marseilles. Farah put her aunt's mind at ease, telling her that neither she nor anyone in the Sutton family believed that she'd done anything wrong, and that they did not think she bore any responsibility for the actions of her former boyfriend.

Raja Noor began to cry as she told Farah that her life had been turned upside down since that time in Marseilles, and that she was now working with a wonderful doctor from the University Hospital, who was helping her regain some of her feelings of self worth. As Farah listened to her aunt's very personal admission of weakness, she noticed that even her dress had changed; she was dressed very conservatively. There was no evidence of cleavage or any other suggestive displays, as was the norm for her. Farah tried to assure her aunt that what she had gone through with Robert was not unique, and that she herself had been controlled by the extreme sexual pleasure that her ex-boyfriend Amin had given to her; she had also been a willing slave to his desires. In addition to her revelations about her mental health, Raja Noor also admitted that she was thinking about having her tattoo removed, but that she had been advised that the pain was worse when you have a tattoo removed. In perhaps an effort to lighten the mood a little, she advised Farah that her breasts seemed to be sagging more, so it wouldn't be long before they hid the entire tattoo.

Farah had to ask her aunt when she'd last talked to Robert, and find out what he had said, but she was not prepared for what her aunt told her next. Robert had phoned her a few weeks earlier, but they hadn't really talked—all he did was tell her that if she said anything bad about him, or if she helped anyone who was trying to hurt him, then she would regret it. When Farah asked what he'd threatened her with, Raja Noor said that he'd told her that he had a video of their night on a yacht in Monte Carlo, and that he would release it to some important people in Malaysia. Farah was curious to know what he was referring to with the yacht, and how she had responded to his threat. Raja Noor said that she and Robert had spent a very intimate evening on a yacht in Monte Carlo, but that she was not aware that someone had been videotaping them. With respect to her response, she advised Farah that she'd told Robert to release the video if he wanted to, as she was going to do everything that she could to see him brought to justice, regardless of what he did. Farah thanked her for her courage and her gesture to help Xavier. As Raja Noor was settling the bill, Farah asked her if she would like to come to her house next week, as she was having the Suttons and Dixon over to experience her first attempt at making bouillabaisse. Raja Noor praised Farah for her courage to undertake such a challenging and specific soup, and then she confirmed that she would be honoured to join her illustrious group for dinner.

THE WEEKEND BEFORE Farah's bouillabaisse reveal, she was working to get her various pieces of art and watercolour prints hung up in her comfortable bungalow, which the Suttons had given to them as a wedding present. Xavier and Farah could certainly not have afforded the four-bedroom house, which was located within one of the most desirable areas of the city, but they knew that Thomas and Mirabel felt better knowing that they were in a nice home in a safe neighbourhood. Farah was fortunate to have Aldia as her faithful assistant, as measuring and hanging pictures required more than one set of hands and one set of eyes. In between pictures, Aldia enjoyed reading some of the letters from Xavier that Farah made available to her, and she also sought Farah's advice on men. She advised Farah that she was in a relationship with a new boyfriend, and since they were getting to a more serious stage, she wanted to know how she should handle that.

"Farah I really would like to hear what you think about the right time to be intimate with your boyfriend. I went through a period when I was too eager and too generous, and I regretted it later."

Farah felt an obligation to let Aldia know that she had been informed by her mother about those times.

"Aldia I should tell you that your mother did share with me her deep concerns during that time, and I was so pleased to hear her say that you had moved past that. But just between you and me, I bet you still have some fond memories of those times."

Aldia had a big smile on her face as she gave Farah a friendly tap.

"I guess you had your wild times also."

Farah could not hide her grin.

"Probably more than I should have."

Farah, who was now more comfortable when she discussed such matters, advised Aldia.

"You should focus more on the compatibility issues with your partner, and not be overtaken by the sex factor."

Aldia was appreciative of the helpful words.

"Thank you so much Farah. I just couldn't talk about these things with my mother."

Farah was reluctant to tell Aldia how much she enjoyed the sexual pleasures of her brother, but she did confirm that sex was an important element in her marriage. As they continued with the picture work, Farah asked Aldia if she would like to bring her boyfriend to the dinner. Aldia first thanked Farah for the kind gesture, then told her that she would need to give it some more thought before deciding whether, or not to invite him.

XAVIER ASKED ANGE if he wanted his leftover apple from lunch, as he knew that Ange had an insatiable appetite, but this time Ange turned him down; his tooth was bothering him, and the apple would only aggravate it. As they sat in their usual place in the prison cafeteria, they could see all the rival gangs congregated around their respective tables, looking as threatening as they could, and hoping that their rivals might think twice about what they might be planning for them.

Ange, who did not need the protection of any gang for his survival, had slowly been educating Xavier on who the controlling forces were, and some of the things he should look for that would indicate that something was going down. Unfortunately for Xavier, the North Africans made up the largest percentage of the population inside Baumettes, and unlike the Marseilles social system—where they often found themselves in low-level positions—they were the ones calling the shots inside the walls of the prison. Ange had been well briefed on Xavier's case, so he knew who the most likely gangs were that might take a shot at him, and he repeatedly reminded Xavier of who they were, and more importantly, how to avoid them. Ange did not take his protected status inside the prison for granted, as he was fully aware that activities and developments on the outside determined what happened on the inside, and he was not always privy to the most current news. Prison for Xavier was survival, and he did not have the luxury of letting his guard down or taking a day off; the system of retribution and revenge within the inmate community never stopped.

FARAH AND ONE of the Suttons' maids were putting in the extra leaf to extend the size of the dining table, but since Xavier and Farah had only four chairs with their dining set, they had to bring in two of the kitchen chairs to accommodate the party of six that Farah was expecting. After setting the cutlery and the various dishes, Farah followed the maid back into kitchen. She tasted the soup, which had been simmering for the past two hours, and, with a big smile on her face, she gave the maid a thumbs up.

Raja Noor was the first to arrive, and she was wearing what appeared to Farah to be a very expensive outfit. Farah also noted that the outfit was, uncharacteristically, very conservative in its design.

Aldia, who had arrived with her parents, but without her new boyfriend, went to the door to let in the late arrival, Dixon, who expressed the standard Kuala Lumpur traffic excuse to his host and to his fellow guests. As Dixon made his way to one of the kitchen chairs that he and Aldia had been assigned, he stopped at Raja Noor's seat, and then he gently put his hands on her shoulders. Raja Noor asked what he was doing, to which Dixon responded that he was checking to make sure that everything was secure. The genuine and forceful laughter resulting from Dixon's answer left Aldia sitting with a perplexed look on her face, as she had obviously not been made aware of Raja Noor's revealing moment on the yacht in Marseilles. When Mirabel informed Aldia about Raja Noor's unveiling, she expressed the same energetic reaction as her fellow dinner mates had.

As the laughter and the playful teasing went on, Farah concentrated on the huge pot of soup, placing it on the serving table in the dining room. She was nervous about how her first attempt at the famous Marseilles dish would be received, but she did not have to wait long to hear the rave reviews from her appreciative guests, including the uninitiated, Aldia.

Everyone was able to talk about Marseilles and the pleasant experiences they had there without feeling guilty, since Xavier was doing well; he had even sent a short note, which Farah read at the end of the soup course.

Farah was handling the pouring and the passing of the coffee to those who had requested a cup, and as she passed one to Thomas, she looked at him and said, "This one is for you, Grandpa."

Everyone went totally quiet. Thomas, confused, asked her what she meant. From the look on Mirabel's face, she knew exactly what Farah was saying—she had previously been made aware of Farah's and Xavier's efforts in Marseilles to get pregnant.

After everyone had extended their congratulations to Farah, and after they had given their suggestions that she take good care of herself, they asked her when she was going to tell Xavier. It was another lovely moment in their successful evening when Farah informed them that she had made Xavier aware of the good news a few days earlier, right after her doctor had confirmed everything for her. Everyone had smiles on their faces as Farah told them that Xavier was over the moon when he heard the news; he had told her that he would start thinking about names, for boys and for girls. When Mirabel heard, she looked over at Thomas and very seriously told him that he had to find a way to get Xavier out of that terrible prison. Thomas indicated to Mirabel that he did not want to say anything just yet, but in view of the news that he was going to be a grandfather, he happily announced that he had just received some very promising news on the Amina situation from Roland. When everyone heard that Amina was now under the protection and control of the Graves Group, and that she had agreed to recant her testimony, they all wanted to know how long it would take before Xavier was exonerated.

Thomas knew that everyone was anxious, but he tried to caution them when he indicated that some issues involving Robert Khoury still needed to be dealt with, and that Graves wanted to get some more certainty on that front before racing to the prosecutor. Thomas quoted Roland as saying that they had just one shot at this, and that they wanted to make sure that everything was in order before they made their definitive move.

Thomas concluded his good news story by saying that it was very likely that Xavier would be assembling baby furniture before too long.

CHAPTER 15

t was the third night, within the last week, when Xavier found himself standing beside Ange's bunk, asking him if he could call for the guards. Ange was experiencing intense pain in his mouth, on and off, but he told Xavier that he did not want to go to the infirmary. He was an old school tough guy who viewed going to the doctor as a sign of weakness; to him, this was worse than suffering the physical pain. He told Xavier that he had had some issues with his teeth in the past, and that he found that if he just put up with the discomfort for a while, it would eventually go away. Xavier could see that this time it was more than just tooth pain, as Ange was sweating profusely. When Ange allowed him to check his forehead, Xavier could feel that he had a fever. He knew he was going to upset Ange as he yelled for a guard, but he was almost certain that if he didn't his cellmate and good friend would die right in front of him.

THE NEXT MORNING, Xavier showed no interest in eating his breakfast, as he moved the different items around the metal tray. He had been unable to get any information from any of the guards on Ange's status. The morning exercise session in the prison yard was a solitary one for Xavier; he found a quiet place at the far end of the soccer field, and he just sat and reflected on another difficult situation that he would have to deal with. Xavier's repeated requests to the guards for information on the health status of his cellmate were met with the standard answer—that he was being looked after—which was of little consolation to him.

His day took a turn for the better, however, when one of the friendly inmates that he had met through Ange's introduction, approached him as they were walking to the afternoon exercise session and told him that Ange had undergone surgery to remove two very badly infected teeth. He was going to be okay. In addition to being the bearer of good news, this inmate also was a member of an inmate soccer team, and his team needed a few extra players. He asked Xavier if he was interested in filling in on their team, as they had an important game against one of their main rivals. Xavier eagerly accepted his invitation, as he missed playing sports, and he remembered that he had at one time been quite proficient at soccer when he'd played at boarding school. He enjoyed the freedom of fighting for the ball and the comfort of knowing that he was part of a team, and his stamina was pretty good, thanks to the fitness regimen that he and Ange had been following.

The joy of playing the game changed for Xavier, however, when a scrum ensued as he was fighting for a loose ball in the corner of the pitch. It seemed as if the players had reacted to a signal, or some indication that it was time to attack. A bunch of the opposing players pounced on Xavier and started to punch and kick him relentlessly. The players on Xavier's team were reluctant to jump in and assist him, as they knew that this attack was personal, and they also knew that they would suffer the same fate if they intervened. They understood very well the laws of survival in Baumettes, and they did not enjoy the same untouchable status that Ange did.

Since the scrum was taking place in the far corner of the pitch, it was not as visible to the guards in the watch towers. As they looked down, they probably told themselves it was just another one of the animal fights, and they just let them go. It was very common for guards to let prisoners work out their differences without interference. Unfortunately for Xavier, this was exactly what was happening this time. When the field level guards finally ordered the scrum to break up, they found the crumpled body of Xavier still on the pitch, writhing in pain.

One of Xavier's friends would report to Ange later that there had been no evidence that the attackers had used knives or shanks; the only sign of blood was from Xavier's broken nose. Xavier was badly bruised and broken, but the attackers had shown some restraint with respect to killer knife blows. Xavier was perhaps saved by the fact that he was a Muslim and that it was a grave sin for a Muslim to kill another Muslim. Xavier's attackers did not appear to have much compassion, based on the severity of the beating they inflicted upon him, but he would have been dead if that was their intention.

ROLAND, AFTER CONSULTING with his superior, Yves, decided to call Thomas Sutton first, instead of Farah, as they felt that Thomas and Mirabel would be able to tell Farah in person, and to provide her with the support that she would need.

Thomas and Mirabel had a difficult time collecting themselves after learning about their son's terrible assault, and not knowing what the prognosis was for him. There was the possibility that he may not survive. Thomas suggested to Mirabel that since it was already three o'clock in the morning, they should wait and drive to Farah's house around the time she would normally be getting up for work. Then they would be able to sit with her and comfort her while they delivered the devastating news.

FROM THE TIME Thomas received the news of Xavier's attack until he and Mirabel were sitting in the back of their van on their way to Farah's house, four hours had passed. Thomas had just finished a telephone conversation with Roland, wherein he'd received additional bad news. The doctors who were treating Xavier had put him into a medically induced coma so that his brain would have a better chance of healing. Thomas had heard of the practice of putting patients with severe brain injuries into a medically induced coma, but he had trouble dealing with the fact that this patient was his one and only son. His distress was heightened by the additional news that Xavier required a respirator to breathe for him, due to the multiple broken ribs and the punctured lung he had sustained. He had other organ trauma as well, and a broken nose. Thomas pushed Roland to give him the doctors' prognosis, but then he wished he had not done so. Roland's response was that Xavier had suffered severe head trauma. This made it difficult for the doctors to predict whether he would live or die, and if he did live if he would have any permanent damage.

Mirabel, who had been listening on the speaker phone as Roland delivered all the devastating news to her husband, tried to control her emotions as she suggested that they tell Farah that Xavier was in critical condition, and that he was receiving the best care possible, which Thomas had been assured was the case. Mirabel reminded Thomas that Farah was pregnant, and that they had an obligation to her and her unborn child, as well as to Xavier, to protect her from any undue stress that could impact her pregnancy. Farah had been paying close attention to her physical and mental health since learning that she was pregnant, and she would need all her physical and her mental strength to help her cope with the news of Xavier's beating.

Mirabel and Farah sat on the sofa in the living room while Thomas, sitting across from them, very thoughtfully released the news to Farah, which enabled her to slowly absorb what had happened to Xavier.

Farah sank back into the sofa and put her hands to her face. Mirabel could see the tears falling beneath her hands, but Farah did not make a noise.

Once Thomas felt it was appropriate, he advised Farah that he had already booked seats for them on the afternoon flight, and he suggested that she pack her things. Farah was clearly shaken up, but she very calmly thanked Thomas, and then she proceeded to her room to get herself ready.

THE AIR FRANCE business class cabin was as empty as it had been when the Suttons and Farah had previously travelled to and from Marseilles. On this trip, however, privacy was not a concern, as the three of them slept the entire flight, or at least tried to, lying with their covers pulled up, contemplating what was waiting for them in Marseilles.

The ICU at the Marseilles hospital looked very modern and very efficiently managed to Farah and the Suttons, as they were escorted by a nurse to Xavier's station.

Farah had told herself that she would not have any outbursts of emotion, but she had to hold back a great deal when she saw her husband lying in his hospital bed with a mass of tubes and hoses and machines hooked up to him. She was transfixed on the various monitors displaying Xavier's various vital signs as Mirabel lovingly directed her to the comfortable visitor chair beside Xavier's bed. Farah knew that Xavier would not be able to see or hear her, but she told Mirabel that she believed that he would be able to sense her presence, and that she was determined to stay by his side for as long as she would be permitted to. She had brought her French textbooks with her, and as she settled into her chair, she pulled them out of her bag, for what looked like it would be a long visit.

Thomas and Mirabel were able to sit down with the lead doctor on Xavier's case and discuss his treatments and his prognosis, as best as the doctor could provide at that time. They were somewhat heartened when the doctor told them that, from his experience, the outcomes for patients in similar situations to the one Xavier was in were largely determined by the internal fight that the patient had in him—or, as he said others had described it, the will to live. Thomas and Mirabel knew that Xavier had always been a fighter, and with the knowledge that he was going to be a father, they were certain that he would be one of those who fought with everything he had.

When Mirabel returned to Xavier's room, she leaned over to tell Farah that it was time for them to go to the hotel and check in, but Farah told her that she was going to stay, and that she would get something from the hospital cafeteria if she got hungry. Mirabel understood that it was the best place for Farah to be at this time, so she reminded her to phone if she needed anything, and then she told her that she and Thomas would be back before the dinner hour.

ROLAND WAS SITTING with Thomas and Mirabel as they waited in the lobby restaurant for Farah, who was refreshing herself after her lengthy stay at the hospital. Farah did not seem to be paying attention when Roland informed them that Yves had successfully convinced the Khalils to meet with him, on the basis that he had information on Robert Khoury that would very likely affect their reputations, and their ability to success-fully operate their business. Thomas was a little confused; he asked Roland why the Khalils were an issue, when they already had Amina in their custody, and since she had already agreed to recant. Roland advised him that Suzanne's office was still trying to arrange for the Marseilles prosecutor to travel to Paris to take Amina's deposition in a Paris courtroom. Amina was reluctant to travel to Marseilles, as she feared that Robert might try to eliminate her before she could testify. With those issues in mind, Roland explained that Yves felt it would be helpful if he could convince the Khalils to use their significant networks and resources to solve the Khoury threat for them. Roland did not admit to Thomas's suggestion that they were trying to get the Khalils to eliminate Robert Khoury, but his sly smile did speak volumes. He assured Thomas that everyone involved in the case at the Graves offices were taking nothing for granted, and they were trying to eliminate any threat or obstacle that they felt might impede Xavier's exoneration.

CHAPTER 16

Yves, a seasoned veteran, had been exposed to many different criminals and crime groups and their operational structures, but after he went through the Khalils' private x-ray unit, before getting patted down and then followed by a team of elite bodyguards, he knew that he was entering the private lair of some big hitters in the arms industry.

Abbas and Asad welcomed Yves warmly, and they let him get comfortable with the cappuccino that their assistant had delivered to him, before asking him to state his case. Yves did not sense any noticeable reactions from either brother, when he told them that Robert was the person who had raped the young lady in Marseilles, resulting in the wrongful conviction of the Malaysian pilot, and that Delorme Aviation was very aware of this position. Yves assumed that the Khalils already knew most of the things that he was telling them. What he wanted to emphasize was that the damage to their business could be mitigated if they stopped protecting Robert Khoury and let him answer for his actions. Or, as Yves put it, let Khoury take the bullet, and save your reputation.

As the brothers sat very comfortably in their plush, leather swivel chairs, Yves could sense that they were considering what he had said, but he also knew that in their world they could never openly admit that.

Abbas asked Yves why he cared so much about Khoury; he suggested that he should be focussing his attention on the young lady who was the victim and on trying to get her to confirm that Khoury was behind the assault and the wrongful conviction. With Amina under his protection, Yves felt comfortable telling the brothers that Amina had already committed to recanting her testimony, but that she was traumatized by the physical and the mental abuse that Khoury had inflicted upon her, and she needed to know that he was no longer a threat. Yves was certain that the brothers had done their homework on him, and that they would have discovered that he had over twenty years with DGSI—French internal security. When he told them that he was fully prepared to facilitate a probe of their business and financial interests in France, they likely took his threat seriously.

Abbas very calmly stood up and thanked Yves for taking the time to come and see them, and then he assured him that they would weigh very carefully everything that he had told them.

Yves had not been expecting the Khalils to say that they would or wouldn't do something. He had just wanted to plant the seed that Robert Khoury was causing them a lot of problems, and that it would be in their best interests to have him stopped.

YVES TURNED ON his phone once his flight landed in Paris, and he saw that he had a voice message from the Grave's employee, Chantelle, who was staying with Amina at the company flat. He was worn out from his long day, so he elected to go straight home to see his wife and deal with the phone message after he'd had a chance to unwind.

Yves was feeling very good about his meeting with the Khalils, as he believed that they would solve the Khoury problem, but after returning the call from Amina's safe house, he realized that Robert Khoury was more of a problem than he had imagined. Chantelle explained to Yves that Amina had received an email which contained images of her in various compromising positions, and that they'd been accompanied by a strong message that if she did not keep her mouth shut the photos would be sent to her father and other members of her family.

Chantelle confirmed that the photos were extremely explicit. Amina had made it very clear that she could not recant her testimony and take the risk that the photos would be released to her family. Yves asked the employee to keep Amina as calm as she could, and to advise her that he would be coming to see her in the next day or two to provide concrete evidence that Robert Khoury was no longer a threat to her.

ROLAND WAS VERY disturbed when he heard of Khoury's threats and Amina's second thoughts, but he told Yves that he thought their plan to involve Raja Noor and the Moroccan General's daughter might just be enough to change her mind back.

Roland wasted little time in contacting both women to ask for their cooperation in setting up Robert Khoury, and, hopefully, bringing him to some form of justice. Both women did not hesitate to provide Roland with current photographs of their tattoos, in the same format as a passport picture is taken, but with the area in the photos extended to include a full view of their breasts and their tattoos. The strategy that Roland and Yves had agreed upon was for Roland to incorporate the photos into mocked-up police filing reports, indicating that they had recently filed charges of sexual assault. They felt that Amina would then realize that she was not the only one suffering at the hands of Robert Khoury, and that she might feel compelled to help them bring him to justice.

The second part of their strategy was to send copies of the mocked-up filing reports to the Khalils, as further inducement for them to act quickly on Robert Khoury. Roland had made Yves aware that if they wanted to ensure that the Khalils believed that the filing documents were real they would have to bring in some specialists, and that would likely delay the process by a few days. Roland and Yves rationalized that, since they had Amina safely in their possession, and with Xavier in the hospital, they could afford to use the extra time to do the job right.

OVER THE LAST three days, Farah had spent most of her time at Xavier's bedside, studying her French and holding one-sided conversations with her comatose husband about their unborn child and the great things they would all do together.

Thomas, or Mirabel, would take over for Farah when they could convince her to return to the hotel to get some healthy food and catch up on valuable sleep, both of which she knew were important for her pregnancy.

On the third day of Farah's bedside vigil, while she was waiting for the orderlies to wheel Xavier back into the room after his brain scan, she was joined by the lead doctor on Xavier's case, who provided her with some much-needed positive news. He informed Farah that Xavier's brain swelling had subsided to the point that they could start to bring him out of his coma. This meant that he would also have the respirator removed, which would enable Xavier to breathe on his own, and he would have the ability to talk.

Farah was overcome with relief and happiness as she stood

up and hugged the doctor. She asked if this news meant that he would make a full recovery. The doctor was careful not to get Farah's expectations too high, but he did say that his brain activity looked normal, and that he didn't believe Xavier's other internal injuries would present any long-term problems for him.

After Farah finished giving Mirabel the wonderful news about Xavier's health, she went over to Xavier and kissed him on his available cheek, telling him that she would be there when he woke up.

Farah now felt comfortable going back to the hotel for the evening, as the doctor had told her that he would only be lucid and able to talk sometime during the next day.

YVES COULD SEE from the look on Amina's face, as he spoke to her about the threat that Robert Khoury had made to her, that she was deathly afraid of her father seeing the explicit photos of her. She was even having difficulty making eye contact with Yves, knowing that he had seen the pictures. He understood her fear, and he had a great deal of empathy. He knew from first-hand dealings with the North African immigrant communities that they viewed these matters in an uncompromising manner. Fortunately for Xavier, Amina was very moved by the two police reports filed by Raja Noor and the Moroccan General's daughter, especially when she saw that they had been subjected to the same personal branding as her. These contributions from the two women were important factors in Amina's agreement to recant her testimony, but the deciding factor was likely the assurance that Yves provided to her, that he had been informed that Robert Khoury was back in Lebanon, and that he was being pursued by people who would have no difficulty removing him as a threat. Earlier, Yves had received a short text message from

Assad Khalil, which simply said, *He is back home now.*

FARAH WAS HOLDING her own with Xavier as they engaged in a French-only conversation, but she was just thrilled that Xavier was sitting up in bed, and that he was showing every sign that he was well on his way to a full recovery. She even joked with him that his nose, which had a slight bump in the middle, made him look tougher, and that she found it very attractive. Xavier and Farah were both fully aware that Amina had sworn an affidavit which recanted her testimony, and they were just awaiting final confirmation from Advocate Suzanne Dupont that the presiding judge had signed off on his full exoneration.

Farah gave Xavier a hug and a lengthy kiss before she said goodbye for the evening, as she was going to attend a dinner that Thomas had organized at the hotel.

Thomas had booked the private dining room in the hotel's main restaurant. He had invited Roland and Yves, as well as Suzanne, to join them for a celebratory dinner, knowing that the paperwork for Xavier's full and complete exoneration was in process, and that Xavier would be discharged from the hospital around the same time.

Thomas had enjoyed his fair share of the fine wine that had been served during their dinner, as had his wife Mirabel, and he was showing some of its effects when he advised the guests that he and his brother James were going to have to sell a lot more frozen baked goods to be able to pay the bills that he had received from Suzanne's office and from the Graves Group.

Jokes notwithstanding, Thomas, Mirabel, and Farah all made sure that Suzanne, Roland, and Yves knew that they would always feel indebted to them for their tireless work in ensuring Xavier's freedom.

XAVIER DID NOT want to leave his sleeping beauty as he looked over at her and remembered their wonderful night, but he had something he needed to do before they returned to Malaysia, and Roland was waiting for him in the lobby.

Xavier had never thought that he would willingly take himself back to Baumettes, but this was a special situation, and he wanted to say goodbye to someone who had possibly saved his life, and who had treated him as good as any good friend could. As he looked through the glass at Ange and reminisced about his time in Baumettes, he had to remind himself that he was talking to someone who did not show his emotions outwardly, as Xavier clearly was, with tears coming down his face. Despite Ange's tough exterior, as they said their final goodbyes, Xavier thought he saw the start of a few tears emerging from the corner of Ange's eyes. Maybe there were tears in Ange's eyes, or maybe Xavier just imagined that there were—only Ange knew the truth.

ONCE XAVIER'S EXONERATION and discharge from the hospital were finalized, the Malaysian government, at the request of the Royal Malaysian Air Force, had agreed to send a special plane to return him and his family to Malaysia. Xavier and his family had discussed the offer, and whether, or not to accept it, in view of the government's complicity in the corruption that had landed Xavier in trouble in the first place. But they had decided that since it was at the request of the Royal Malaysian Air Force, they should be honoured to accept.

Xavier and his family enjoyed the long flight in the luxurious comfort of the large government jet, normally used by the Prime Minister and his senior Cabinet Ministers for official trips abroad.

When Farah woke up from her lengthy sleep, and she saw that Xavier was not in his seat, she asked Thomas where he was. Thomas informed her that he had gone into the back part of the cabin to change. Farah was a little perplexed as to why he would be changing one hour before they landed, but when he appeared in his full military outfit, she thought that he must know something she didn't.

Farah looked out of her side window as they made their descent into Subang Air Base and noticed that there was a crowd of people congregated by the entrance way to the VIP terminal. Then she understood.

After the stairs had been affixed to the front exit of the plane, the door swung open, and Captain Xavier Sutton, accompanied by his lovely wife Farah and his proud parents, was welcomed home by the chiefs of all four military branches, to the sounds of a full military band.

Farah's pilot had returned home, and his country wanted to thank him for enduring the great injustice that he had suffered while faithfully serving his country.

Printed in Canada